"Don't give up and I will help you."

The voice continued, "I am Princess Amonit, daughter of Rameses the Fifth, Pharaoh of all Egypt."

I couldn't have dropped my hand to my lap faster if the beads had been red-hot. Had they really spoken?

"What is it?" Rev asked beside me.

I glanced nervously at him.

"What?" he asked again. "Marina, your face just lost every trace of color."

"Ah...you didn't hear something, did you? Sort of a—er—a voice?"

Rev's handsome face took on the same expression it had had in the L.A. museum. Back when I'd told him I'd seen a bird with a human head in the exhibit case. I stared at him, hoping he didn't think I should be committed.

Having a vivid imagination was one thing. But hearing voices?

Maybe I was crazy!

Dear Reader,

Inspiration for *The Mummy Case* struck when I was
admiring the beads worn by another writer at a
conference banquet. It turned out they were mummy
beads that the woman had found on a trip to Egypt.
"Of course," she'd explained, "they aren't real."

All I could think about was how spooky it might feel to
wear those beads if they *were* genuine. What if they'd
actually once been worn by a mummy? From that event,
I began to formulate the idea for *The Mummy Case,*
in which my heroine, Marina Haine, does wear such
beads . . . and they begin to speak to her!

I hope you will be as intrigued by the beaded necklace in
The Mummy Case as I was by the ones that inspired
this story and the sequel to follow in February,
The Mummy Beads.

Sincerely,

Dawn Stewardson

THE
MUMMY
CASE

Dawn Stewardson

Harlequin Books

TORONTO • NEW YORK • LONDON
AMSTERDAM • PARIS • SYDNEY • HAMBURG
STOCKHOLM • ATHENS • TOKYO • MILAN
MADRID • WARSAW • BUDAPEST • AUCKLAND

To Mary Jo Putney,
who was wearing the beads which
inspired this book

And to John, always

ISBN 0-373-22257-2

THE MUMMY CASE

Copyright © 1994 by Dawn Stewardson.

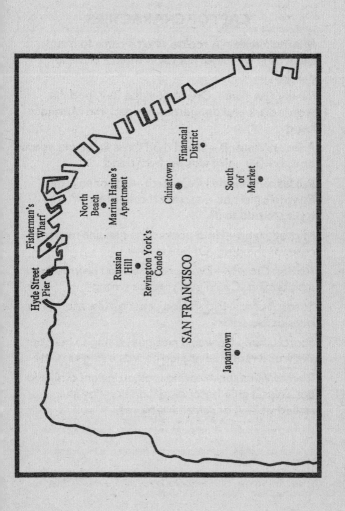

Hyde Street
Pier

Fisherman's
Wharf

North
Beach

Marina Haine's
Apartment

Russian
Hill

Revington York's
Condo

Chinatown

Financial
District

South
of
Market

SAN FRANCISCO

Japantown

CAST OF CHARACTERS

Marina Haine—A rookie when it came to fraud, she was in way over her head when it came to murder.

Revington York—One look at the Rev, and the words *dark and dangerous* popped into Marina's head.

Princess Amonit—She'd died three thousand years ago, but her spirit was far from dead.

Professor Heinrich Reinhardt—Rumor said the Egyptologist had a secret art collection. Was he trying to add to it?

Mickey Flynn—He'd packed the genuine mummy case for shipping. Or had he?

Ashton Crawly—Everyone suspected he was the mastermind. Could everyone be wrong?

Susan Dafoe—Did she look enough like Marina to pass as her sister?

Scott Usher—He was a nice guy, trying to help out. But was it really Revington he was trying to help?

Rachel Windsor—Marina took an instant dislike to her. Was it only because of the sexy way she smiled at Rev, or something more?

Chapter One

Whatever I expected when Charlie Obregon ordered me into his office Monday morning, it sure wasn't his saying, "Marina, Nat Fishbein had a heart attack over the weekend. He's in San Francisco General."

I was glad Charlie had told me to sit down before dropping his bombshell, because I felt suddenly hollow.

It was six weeks since I'd moved from boring old Auto Claims into Special Claims. And each working day of those six weeks, I'd been tagging along after Nat Fishbein while he tried to teach me everything he knew about investigating fraudulent insurance claims.

"Is he going to...?" The final words stuck in my throat, but Charlie was waving his pudgy hand dismissively.

"*Minor* heart attack. Really nothing more than a little pain and an irregular heartbeat. He'll be back to normal in no time."

That made me feel better, although I didn't think Charlie should be trying to make even a minor heart attack sound like a case of the flu.

"But of all the times he could have picked," Charlie muttered. "He's left me up to my butt in investigations and down to the dregs in staff."

The dregs. Nice, I thought. Not that I had any delusions about being an ace investigator yet, but the remark was hardly a boost to my ego.

I dismissed it as typical Charlie and glanced at the pile of folders on his desk. He wasn't exaggerating about how much work was stacked up in the department. That pile was so high he could stand up and still hide his entire five-foot-three frame behind it.

At Sherwin McNee Indemnity of California, anything that has even a whiff of fraudulence about it gets turned over to Special Claims. Special being a euphemism for suspicious. And lately, there'd been so many claims referred to the fraud squad, as everyone else in the company calls us, that all of Charlie's experienced investigators were overloaded.

"Okay, here's the deal," he said. "You heard about that museum exhibit thing last Thursday night?"

"You mean all the excitement at the Donner opening?"

Charlie gave me a withering look that asked what else could he possibly have been referring to.

"Of course I heard about it," I said lamely. Maybe his dregs remark hadn't been so far off base. The Donner exhibit fiasco seemed to be all people were talking about, especially after the way the news media had gone to town.

They'd reported the theft of a three-thousand-year-old Egyptian mummy case, complete with mummy, as a distinctly bizarre crime, and had played the story for all it was worth.

"It's ours," Charlie said.

"Excuse me?"

"The old coffin. The mummy case," he snapped as if I were feebleminded. "I just got handed the file. Sherwin McNee issued a policy to cover the exhibit while it was on loan to the Donner. The museum called us about it first thing Friday, but General Claims sat on it over the weekend. Bunch of idiots in that department. They should have known the minute it came in to pass it on to us."

Mentally, I raced through what I recalled from the news coverage. A museum in Los Angeles had loaned an exhibit of ancient Egyptian artifacts to the Donner, here in San Francisco. The gem of the collection was what Charlie had referred to as the old coffin. The gilded, jewel-encrusted case that contained the mummy of an Egyptian princess.

But at the exhibit's opening, some expert from the museum in L.A. had realized that the case on display was a forgery, not the priceless piece that had left *his* museum.

"Our coverage went into effect," Charlie was saying, "the minute that exhibit was loaded into the moving van in L.A. So regardless of whether the fake was substituted en route, or after it got here, we're on the hook unless the original is recovered. And we're talking a multimillion-dollar claim."

My excitement level was rising fast. Fraud squad rookies like me don't normally get handed multimillion-dollar claims to investigate. We get cars that were driven off bridges by their owners, then reported as stolen. Or accidental fires, with gasoline cans left at the scene.

But Charlie would only be talking to me about the mummy case claim because he was giving it to me.

"The police seem to be dragging their feet on this," he said. "And I can't afford to let the trail get any colder without starting our preliminary investigation. I would have put Nat to work on it, but with him out of commission, I'll have to get things going myself."

My excitement level crashed to ground zero. Charlie was going to handle the case himself? I'd heard it had been well over twenty years since he'd done any field work. Mainly he offered suggestions on how to handle the cases he assigned his staff.

And remembering a few cryptic remarks Nat had dropped, I was pretty sure Charlie had *never* been a crack investigator. I even recalled one comment suggesting our boss had frequently fumbled the ball when he was called in to play.

But he'd always had a talent for theorizing and organization. Kicking him up into administration had been a smart move.

"You can give me a hand on this," he was saying. "After six weeks, you should be able to cope with the basics of preliminary investigation on your own."

On my own? Charlie was going to let me loose on my own? Well, that was more like what I'd been hoping he'd say. Even if I *would* just be giving him a hand.

I tried not to look thrilled, but I obviously failed because he glared across his desk at me and shook his bald head. "Don't get overexcited, Haine. I said *basics*."

Switching to people's last names was a sure sign he was annoyed, so I nodded quickly.

"And don't get the idea I actually believe you're ready to work alone. You aren't. But you're all I've got. So take this," he went on, tossing over the top folder from his stack.

I grabbed it before it could slide off his desk, then focused on him again.

"Read through the background material Research put together. I'm going to head over to the Donner and start talking to people there, see what I can get from them. You begin by checking out the guy in that file. He's known as The Rev, and my first impression tells me he's the most obvious one to have planned the heist. Which makes him our initial prime suspect."

"The Rev? Our prime suspect is a minister?"

The question earned me one of Charlie's patented "are you an idiot?" glances. "The Rev," he said, "is one Mr. Revington York. He owns Careful Wheels. A company that transports things needing special care."

"Like museum exhibits," I guessed, hoping to redeem myself.

"Exactly. Including our Egyptian exhibit. And The Rev knows a lot of people in the art world. Artists, craftsmen, restorers."

"The kind of people who could create an excellent forgery."

"Right."

"And what about lead time?" I asked, racking my brain to think of the questions that would have rolled easily off Nat's tongue. "That mummy case couldn't have been duplicated overnight."

"Revington York had time," Charlie said. "The Donner arranged months ago for him to handle the exhibit shipment."

"And any ideas on motive? Anything obvious?"

Asking that actually made Charlie smile approval. I silently thanked Nat Fishbein for his teaching.

"Motive," Charlie repeated. "The Rev's company has been having serious cash-flow difficulties. I think

Careful Wheels might even be at risk of rolling into bankruptcy. So could be The Rev decided to take care of his problems by substituting a fake mummy in a reproduction of the case, and selling the genuine goods on the black market.''

I nodded. According to Nat, there were a lot of wealthy private art collectors who had no ethical problems with buying hot works of art or artifacts.

''Remember,'' Charlie said, ''all I want from you is preliminary fact-finding. Just go over to Careful Wheels and see what you can learn without being obvious. Even if The Rev wasn't behind things, that mummy case could have been switched in transit. And if it was, we can get him for negligence.''

I nodded again. If the substitution had been made while the real case was on its way to San Francisco, Revington York's insurance company would be liable for at least part of the settlement. That would save Sherwin McNee Indemnity a pile of money.

''And don't make a single move without consulting me first,'' Charlie added. ''The minute I can free up someone else, I'll have him take over from you.''

I considered drawing his attention to the matter-of-fact way he'd used the pronoun *him,* but decided not to bother. He already knew he was sexist. He just didn't care.

Charlie pushed himself up from his chair, signaling we were finished. ''And Marina,'' he said as I started toward the door, ''for God's sake, don't screw up.''

WITH CHARLIE'S SOLID VOTE of nonconfidence ringing in my ears, I'd taken the file to the drab little cubicle that served as my office and started through the material.

At first there didn't seem to be a whole lot of information I hadn't already read in the newspapers or seen on TV. I knew that the mummy case actually belonged to a private collector. It had been at the L.A. museum for years, though, on permanent loan. Aside from that, the file material mostly served to jog my memory about the names of the players and the details of what had happened.

The Donner Museum's core collection is Indian art of the Pacific Coast region, but it mounts two or three special exhibits each year.

The pieces for the Egyptian exhibit had been loaned by the Los Angeles Museum of Historic Art, and its Chief Egyptologist, Professor Heinrich Reinhardt, was the expert who'd blown the whistle.

He'd been invited to San Francisco for the opening, and the instant the mummy case was unveiled, he'd strongly suspected it was a forgery, not the priceless piece that had left L.A.

A subsequent comparison of the case on display with old photographs of the *real* one had proven him right. The mummy case at the Donner was a fake. And X rays of the mummy inside proved she wasn't Princess Amonit.

For one thing, the princess had been buried wearing jewelry. And she'd had over a hundred amulets tucked into the folds of her linen wrappings. The phony mummy had none of these.

There hadn't been many specifics about the mummy itself in the news—only that the one in the case wasn't the princess who belonged there.

I'd simply assumed someone had substituted one ancient mummy for another, so reading the detailed facts now sent such a shiver up my spine that it left the hairs on the back of my neck standing on end.

The vintage of the mummy in the phony case was as recent as that of the case itself.

I had trouble making myself read on past that point. I could accept someone, obviously a very talented someone, creating a reproduction of the mummy case. It was the same principal as forging a painting.

But somebody had actually mummified a modern woman to substitute for Princess Amonit, using a process similar to the original Egyptian one. Her body had been packed in salt to dry it out, then thoroughly soaked in bitumen and wrapped in strips of linen. But who was she?

Were we talking body snatchers here, as well as antiquity forgers? Or worse yet, were we talking murderers? That wouldn't be established until an autopsy had been done and the cause of death determined. But the report set forth murder as a definite possibility.

That hadn't even been suggested on the news. Until they knew for sure that they were dealing with a murder, the police didn't like that sort of rumor floating around. And no wonder. Just the thought of running into a murderer while working on this investigation had me on edge.

I reminded myself I'd only be involved on a preliminary level. And that murder was merely a possibility. Besides, if we *were* talking murder . . . well, that was for the police, not insurance adjusters, to deal with.

I firmly turned the page face down and concentrated on what I came to next. An envelope containing a brief bio and candids of our prime suspect, Mr. Revington York.

The Rev was tall and lean, with blue eyes and dark hair that was a little too long, a straight nose that was a little too big, and eyebrows that were a little too heavy. In every one of the pictures, he sported a five-o'clock shadow that looked more like an eight-o'clock shadow.

He wasn't exactly unattractive, but he certainly wasn't my type. I prefer my men clean-cut and freshly shaven.

Which was not relevant, I told myself. The guy was a suspect.

"Marina?"

I glanced up at the sound of Charlie's voice. He was standing outside my cubicle, his suit jacket slung over his shoulder. From the angle I was sitting at, he looked like an only slightly overgrown elf.

"I'm on my way to the Donner," he said. "Just wanted to tell you again to check every step with me before you take it. Give me a call at the museum after you've talked to The Rev. Security will track me down for you. We'll see how things go at Careful Wheels, then I'll decide what you should do next. And remember, for God's sake—"

"Don't screw up," I interrupted, unable to resist.

"Right," Charlie said. "This is a high-profile case. And if you make me look bad, you'll be back in Auto Claims so fast your head will spin."

I was tempted to thank him for being so supportive, but I didn't. The only sarcasm Charlie appreciates is his own.

He started off down the hall, leaving me trying not to think about the gruesome prospect of ending up back in Auto Claims. I had no intention of screwing up. And if I did a good job on the preliminary investigation, maybe Charlie wouldn't be so determined to have someone else take over from me.

Quickly, I began reading through The Rev's bio. Revington York was thirty-two. Like me, single. Unlike me, into sailing. Every time I get too close to San Francisco Bay, my stomach feels queasy.

He lived downtown, owned a condo on Russian Hill. Definitely a good address.

It wasn't all that far from my apartment in North Beach, but the neighborhoods are very different. North Beach is less pricy and more European. In fact, a lot of people still call it Little Italy. It's been invaded, though, by numerous artists, poets and free spirits, and I like the flavor they add.

There wasn't anything else of real interest in The Rev's bio, just some basic info on his habits, so I opened the other envelope in the file.

Inside it were a dozen nine-by-twelve color glossies of the mummy cases, six of the authentic one and six of the forgery, with the almost imperceptible differences circled in red. There was also written material on both the cases and the princess. I set the pictures aside for more detailed study and began reading.

Princess Amonit had lived in Egypt's Age of Ramses, 1292 to 1075 B. C. She'd been the daughter of Ramses V, and her age at death was estimated as twenty-eight—coincidentally, exactly my present age.

The case, just a touch over five feet in length, was the inner coffin that had originally rested inside a stone sarcophagus. The princess might have been my age, but she'd certainly been much shorter than my five-foot-six inches.

The information sheet went on to describe the authentic case in detail, but I switched my attention to the photographs.

A full-length shot from the top revealed the mummy case was a beautiful, larger-than-life, hollow wooden statue of the princess, with a vast amount of inlay. And the close-up of her painted face was so lifelike...suddenly, an incredibly spooky feeling seized me as I realized lifelike wasn't all it was.

Gazing at her face was almost like looking at a painting of myself.

I sat staring blankly at the close-up for several minutes before my mind began working again. I'm not normally a believer in the paranormal. But the fact that Princess Amonit, who lived three thousand years ago, had looked amazingly like me, really started me wondering.

Could something far bigger than Charlie—no wisecrack about his height intended—have taken a hand in getting me involved with this claim?

I glanced at Amonit's face again, thinking maybe my imagination was working overtime, but it wasn't. There was definitely a close resemblance between us. It was partly due to her long, dark, straight hair, of course. Aside from my bangs, the simple style was the same.

But she also had dark eyes like mine, a too-full mouth that the odd kind man told me was lush, and the same highly defined bone structure people said made me photogenic. Not that you'd believe it from my driver's license picture.

I forced my eyes from Amonit's face and went back to the full-length shot. The wooden surface of the mummy case, more or less the shape of a woman's body, was covered with horizontal rows of hieroglyphics, emphasized by heavy gilding. The case was inset, here and there, with emeralds and rubies—particularly the area around Amonit's neck and shoulders.

Even without considering the antiquity factor, it would be easy to believe Sherwin McNee Indemnity was looking at paying a multimillion-dollar claim. At least, it would be if the real mummy case wasn't recovered. And my job was to help ensure it was.

Putting everything back in the folder, I slipped it into the super-large shoulder bag I'd bought a few weeks ago, checking that my snub-nosed .38 was carefully secured in the zippered compartment.

Having it there still made me nervous. Despite the way I'd laughed off my parents' worries about the safety of my new job, being licensed to carry a gun was a constant reminder that Special Claims work could be dangerous.

Once organized, I started for the underground parking garage and my trusty old Mustang. Its gold paint no longer shines and it doesn't have all the jazzy features of newer models, but I have no intention of replacing it until I have to.

Most important, it's paid for. And secondly, even though San Francisco's hills are hell on cars, so far this one has never let me down.

Outside, the sun had broken through the morning fog earlier than usual, so I opened my sunroof to the July warmth and headed for the Mission district, where Careful Wheels was located.

San Francisco General sat on the edge of that neighborhood, and I started thinking that maybe after I'd checked out Revington York I'd stop by and visit Nat. On second thought, though, I decided that in case his heart attack hadn't been quite as minor as Charlie had claimed, I'd phone first.

Mission is not the best place for a woman on her own. But on top of acquiring a gun, I'd begun taking self-defense classes—a departmental requirement. Besides, during the day, the worst I'd likely face would be a few whistles and suggestive remarks.

I drove slowly along South Van Ness, watching for the side street that Careful Wheels was on. By this point, I'd thought up several innocent-sounding questions I could ask The Rev and had gone on to think about possible opening lines.

None of them sounded quite right, and I suddenly wished Nat, with his thirty years of experience, was sitting beside me. After six solid weeks in his company, I felt a little lonely without him.

A little lonely and more than a little insecure. I desperately didn't want to screw up. Charlie didn't make idle threats, so I knew he'd meant what he'd said about bouncing me back to Auto Claims. And that would be my own special version of a fate worse than death.

THE CAREFUL WHEELS building was an old, three-story frame warehouse that could have used a paint job. It had a parking lot on one side with two moving vans in it. The shiny, clean white vehicles with sedate black lettering looked a lot more impressive than the building.

I paused outside the front door, took a deep breath, then walked into the reception area, which was done in all-over beige with minimal furniture. There was a filing cabinet and a large desk that threatened to overflow with papers. At the moment, it was devoid of a person.

Behind that, the wall was covered with huge, scrawled-on calendar sheets. One for each of the next several months. The scrawling probably represented upcoming jobs.

A door toward one end of the wall stood half open, and I could see it led into an office. Just as I was deciding whether to call out or walk over and knock, a man jerked the door fully open.

It was Revington York. Tall, dark-haired and lean. With an eight-o'clock shadow at eleven in the morning.

He stood glaring at me from the doorway, his eyes blue ice. At least, the way he was glaring was icy. And blue-eyed or not, one look at him and the words *dark* and *dangerous* popped into my head.

I mentally shoved them aside, but there was something unnerving about him, some kind of hard-edged masculine magnetism that those photographs Research had provided hadn't captured.

Every so often, my intuition clicks in about someone, and this was one of those times. I knew I was going to have trouble dealing with Mr. Revington York.

I tried telling myself there was no reason to feel so uneasy. Even if The Rev *was* a criminal, he was into art forgery. Creative crime, not violence.

Then the imaginary little voice in my head, which always feels free to speak up, said, "Don't forget about that modern woman someone mummified...and maybe murdered first."

I swallowed uncomfortably. I'd have liked nothing better than to have forgotten that little detail. But murder was only a possibility, I reminded myself. And it was one I was going to do my utmost not to think about.

"You're late," The Rev said at last, his tone distinctly unfriendly.

Oh, Lord! Nat had been right. Charlie *was* a bit of a bumbler when it came to field work. He'd let Revington York know I was coming here without telling me.

"I told Timely Temps nine, and it's after eleven," he said a little less sharply. "Is that what your company considers timely?"

"Ahh . . . I think there's a mix-up here," I managed to say. "I'm not from Timely Temps. I'm from Sherwin McNee Indemnity Insurance."

"Oh. Well, thanks for stopping by, but I've got all the insurance I need," he said, starting to turn back into his office.

"No, wait, you don't understand, Mr. York. You *are* Mr. Revington York, aren't you?" I added quickly, realizing he might wonder how I seemed so sure of his identity.

"I...I'm supposed to ask you some questions, then," I mumbled when he nodded. So much for all my carefully thought-out opening lines.

"About the museum exhibit you shipped from L.A. to the Donner," I persisted. "We're the company that insured it." Nat, I reflected ruefully, would have been handling this at least a hundred times better than I was.

"Oh, jeez," The Rev muttered, running his fingers through his too-long hair. "Look, my secretary has been calling in sick since the start of last week. This is the third morning that the temp I expected didn't show. And I've already spent hours going over everything with the cops. Didn't you people and the police get together on this?"

"Of course we did."

He seemed dubious, so I firmly said, "We *do* cooperate with each other. But there are things the company has to check out directly. In case we have to settle with the Donner, we need information from you for our reports."

"Can't your reports wait? This isn't a good time for me."

"I'm afraid I've got to talk to you now. People forget details. Facts get confused. So I was told to interview everyone involved as soon as possible. I'm sorry... it's my job."

The Rev looked extremely unhappy, but he stepped aside and gestured me into his office.

He didn't step aside very far, though, and I had to pass by close enough that I could smell the distinctly masculine scent of the man. Just a hint of woodsy after-shave mingled with a raw earthiness that hadn't come from a bottle.

His inner sanctum was as unremittingly beige as the outer office. The dark blue shirt and jeans he was wearing were all that offered a break from the monochromatic decor.

"By the way, I'm Marina Haine," I said, extending my hand.

He gave it a fast, hard shake, then nodded toward the sole visitor's chair.

While he sank into the chair behind his desk, I dug around in my bag and produced a card. Before handing it over, I remembered to double-check that it was one identifying me simply as a Sherwin McNee Indemnity representative, not one that specified I was with the Special Claims Department.

He inspected the card so closely I began to worry that I should have triple-checked it.

"Well," he said, finally putting it down, "exactly what do you want to know?"

I smiled anxiously across the desk. The confusing start we'd gotten off to had left me extremely rattled, and every question I'd thought up earlier had vanished from my brain.

"It might be easiest," I said when none of them magically reappeared, "if you just tell me everything that happened. Then I'll only have to ask about any gaps that you could maybe fill in."

"Tell you everything that happened?" he repeated, a trace of a grin stealing across his face. It deepened the crinkly lines beside his eyes and melted some of their blue ice.

"Everything *I* know about what happened," he went on, "takes about thirty seconds to tell. The staff of the museum in L.A. crated the pieces we were to bring up to San Francisco, and two of my guys went down there to get them. Two guys who have been with me since I started Careful Wheels," he added pointedly. "Two guys who are bonded."

I nodded to let him know I wasn't missing the point.

"So, my guys loaded the crates into one of our vans and locked it up tight. Then they drove nonstop from L.A. to here, backed the van up to the receiving dock at the Donner and unloaded the crates into the museum. End of what happened that I know anything about. Until the exhibit opening, when all hell broke loose."

"They drove nonstop?" I said. "All the way from L.A. to San Francisco? Over four hundred miles?"

The Rev shrugged. "Okay, maybe with a couple of pit stops. Ten minutes each, tops. And when we're moving valuable cargo like that exhibit, both men never leave the van at the same time. One is always in the cab."

"And the one in the cab?" I tried, hoping I wasn't giving myself away. "Can he see the rear of the van? I mean, could something have been going on back at the doors that he didn't know about?"

"The doors were locked."

"Yes, you mentioned that. But if someone, somehow, had a key?"

"No one had a key who shouldn't have had. Look, Ms. Haine," he said, leaning across the desk, his eyes pure ice again, "I've already talked to *my* insurance people. So I know how much you'd like me to say it's possible I could have been at fault. That it's possible the mummy case was taken from my van. But it wasn't. There's no way."

I nodded slowly. Revington York *would* try to convince me his story was true. Because if the switch *had* been made in his van, if *his* insurance company got stuck paying part of a multimillion-dollar claim, his premiums would skyrocket.

Or worse yet for him, the company would cancel his policy. If that happened, he'd have trouble getting coverage elsewhere. And no insurance coverage would mean the end of his business.

"Sorry," he muttered, when the phone began to ring. "I'll have to take this. No secretary."

I glanced around the room, once he'd picked up, pretending not to listen. But after his initial greeting, there wasn't much to listen to, anyway.

Whoever had called was doing ninety-nine percent of the talking, so I stopped pretending and glanced back at Revington York. Instantly, I wished I hadn't.

He was gazing directly at me, looking as if breaking my neck would give him extreme pleasure.

"Yeah," he said into the phone, scribbling something on a piece of paper without looking away from me. "Yeah, I'd say that's pretty obvious, all right. Well, listen, thanks a lot. I really owe you for this."

I tried smiling as he hung up, but it did nothing to make him look less angry.

"So..." he said, picking my card up again. "Ms. Haine...representative from Sherwin McNee Indemnity. That was a friend of mine who just called. A good friend. He works at the Donner Museum."

I nodded, feeling sick. My intuition had certainly been right. I'd been having trouble dealing with Mr. Revington York since the moment I'd arrived. And whatever his good friend had just told him clearly wasn't going to help.

"Some guy showed up there from your company an hour or two ago," he went on. "Some guy who's asking questions. And a whole lot of them are about me. A fat, bald, midget of a guy named..."

He paused, glancing down at what he'd scribbled. "Named Charlie Obregon. A vice president at Sherwin McNee. In charge of what my friend referred to as your company's fraud squad. He anybody you know?"

"Ahh...he's my boss," I admitted, feeling like a pinned bug, skewered to my chair by The Rev's glare.

"I see." Revington York tapped the edge of his desk with my card a few times. "So I guess," he eventually said, "if this guy is your boss, that would make you more a fraud 'squadette' than just a simple representative.

"And I also guess," he added, leaning forward with a menacing expression, "you know why this boss of yours has apparently decided *I* was the brains behind the mummy case switch. So let's hear the explanation."

Chapter Two

I tried to think of brilliant words to convince The Rev he wasn't really our prime suspect, regardless of whatever dumb questions Charlie was asking at the Donner.

When nothing brilliant came to mind, I searched for words that would at least beat total gibberish.

Still nothing. Undoubtedly, the problem lay in the way Revington York was glaring at me with murderous intent. It was, to put it mildly, highly unnerving.

"If you work for this fraud squad guy," he snarled when I said nothing, "then you didn't come here just to ask me a few questions for some damned report, did you?"

"Ahh...actually, I did." My voice sounded squeaky, so I cleared my throat before going on. "That's all Charlie Obregon told me to do. Just ask a few questions."

"Uh-uh. You came here hoping I'd let something slip and incriminate myself, didn't you? And why the hell does this shrimpy boss of yours suspect me, anyway?"

I had an awfully strong suspicion that I shouldn't even open my mouth again, but I also have an awfully strong instinct for survival. And with every passing second, Revington York was looking more like he was about to come over his desk and strangle me.

That meant keeping quiet might not be in my best interest. Besides, he'd already figured out exactly what was what, so my denying it would only make me sound like a fool—despite Charlie's theory that you should never admit *anything* to a suspect.

"Well," I finally said, praying Charlie wouldn't ask for details about this session, "it's not *exactly* that Charlie suspects you. Not seriously, I mean. It's just that we have to consider every possibility. And your company *did* have possession of the mummy case for ten hours or so. And you *did* know you'd be shipping the exhibit long enough in advance that . . . that having a reproduction made would have been possible."

"Dammit to hell!" The Rev slammed his desk for emphasis, making me jump a good foot. "I didn't have a thing to do with what happened. And that switch wasn't made while my guys had the case."

"Then when do you think it was made?" I asked, almost surprised when my voice still worked.

"How the hell do I know? Maybe the phony was what got crated in L.A. Or maybe the substitution was made after it was delivered to the Donner. Sometime after that but before the opening," he added as if I had a negative IQ.

I gave myself a mental slap on the wrist. The possibility that the genuine article had never left L.A. hadn't occurred to me, and it certainly should have. But I'd been so excited at the prospect of working on this, I'd focused entirely on the options Charlie had tossed out: that the switch had either been made en route or after the exhibit reached San Francisco.

But the other possibility would have occurred to Charlie. And since he hadn't even mentioned it, he must have had a reason for rejecting it right off. I'd have to ask him about that.

"Listen," The Rev was saying, "do you think I'm a lunatic? That if I'd actually had anything to do with stealing the mummy case, I'd have had it taken from my own moving van? I've got Careful Wheels' reputation to consider. And what the hell are people going to think, with your damned boss running around implying I planned the whole thing? If he's never heard of slander, he will have by the time my lawyer's finished talking to him."

I winced. I hadn't had time to decide whether I should tell Charlie about that phone call The Rev had gotten or not, but now I definitely had to. In case Revington York was serious about the lawyer bit, I'd have to warn Charlie.

"Somebody has to shut the guy up before he ruins my reputation," The Rev was muttering.

Glancing uneasily at him, I tried to tell if he was still thinking about calling his lawyer, or if he'd moved on to thinking about other ways of shutting Charlie up. As a fan of old gangster movies, I've heard people talk about shutting guys up a million times. And they usually mean permanently.

"I'm sure," I offered, "that Charlie isn't trying to ruin your reputation, Mr. York. I'm sure he's only—"

"I don't care what he's *trying* to do. I care that if he gets people even wondering if I *might* have been involved, I'll lose credibility. My business is transporting valuable items. You think people are going to trust me with valuable items if they figure I'm a crook? This guy just can't go wandering around a museum asking questions about me."

"Well . . . asking questions is kind of our job. Charlie's only trying to make sure the real mummy case is recovered."

"And that's *your* job, too? That's what you're supposed to be doing? Finding out who was behind the switch so the real case gets recovered?"

I nodded. Of course, he was making me sound like more of a major player in this than I actually was, but—

"Fine. Then I'll help you."

His words hung in the air for a moment before they registered. "Excuse me?" I said when they did.

"You figure out who was actually responsible and my name is in the clear, right? You eliminate the possibility that anyone at Careful Wheels was involved and my insurance company relaxes, right?"

I nodded again, but most of my brain was still dealing with The Rev's proposal. My prime suspect offering to help me was absolutely ludicrous. I might be new at this game, but even *I* recognized ludicrous when it looked me in the face.

"Fine," Revington snapped as if my nodding had meant I'd agreed to his suggestion. "Then we'll work together, because with your boss running around muddying my name all to hell, the faster this is sorted out the better."

"Look, Mr. York, I can see why you'd like everything cleared up, but my working with you just isn't feasible."

"Why not? I know people at the museums both here and in L.A. And you're a detective. You figure out the questions to ask and I'll know who to put them to. It's a good idea, right?"

He was wearing that "come over the desk at me" expression again, so I resisted the impulse to tell him his idea was the pits. Instead, I said, "Let's just slow down for a minute," then waited until he leaned back an inch.

"First off," I went on, "I'm not a detective. I'm an insurance adjuster."

"With this fraud squad division."

"Well . . . yes."

"And how long have you worked for Sherwin McNee?"

"Four years, but I've only—"

"That's plenty long enough. So I give you what help I can and you solve the crime. You end up looking good and everyone knows I had nothing to do with the theft. We both win, right?"

"No, Mr. York—"

"You can call me Rev," he said, flashing me the first smile I'd seen outside of his photos.

It was, I noted with surprise, a very nice smile. He didn't look even faintly homicidal when he smiled. But I recalled once reading that the Boston Strangler had a very nice smile, too.

"Look," I tried again. "I've been at Sherwin McNee for four years, but I spent most of it checking out auto thefts and traffic accidents. I've only been in Special Claims for six weeks. In fact, this is the first time they've let me out on my own."

The minute I said that I realized I should have phrased it differently. Not only had I screwed up this meeting, now I was sounding as if I'd spent my life in a home for the terminally dumb.

The news about my rookie status had taken the shine off Revington York's smile, and he sat rubbing his eight-o'clock shadow thoughtfully.

"You still know more about investigations than I do," he said at last. "All that auto stuff had to teach you something. And six weeks on this fraud squad is better than nothing."

He reached over and switched his answering machine on, saying, "Good thing this is a quiet day. And my secretary swears she'll be in tomorrow. She can hold the fort then. So let's get started. Where do we begin?"

"*We* don't begin. Look, this is *my* job, not yours. I can't just team up with a civilian." Especially not a civilian who, despite his protests, could be guilty as sin. All crooks protest their innocence—Nat Fishbein's number one guiding rule.

"Well, what the hell am I supposed to do while you and your boss are running around asking questions?" Rev demanded. "You listen to me, Marina Haine, I'm damned well not sitting still while you people ruin my reputation. Not when I can help prove you're all wet."

"But, I—"

"And now that I know you're just a beginner," he interrupted, shaking his head in an extremely exaggerated way, "I'd be left worrying that you might miss something important. Something *I* would pick up on because I know how museums work. And because I know a lot of the people who were involved with organizing this exhibit. So I'm going to help you. Whether you like the idea or not."

I shrugged my bag onto my shoulder and stood up. Trying to reason with the man was pointless. "I'm sorry I took so much of your time," I muttered, turning toward the door.

"Marina?"

I glanced back.

"Marina, what would happen if I called this boss of yours? Tore a strip off him about sending someone over here who came straight out and accused me of being guilty? Tried to badger me into confessing?"

"I didn't do that!"

Revington York leaned back in his chair, lazily clasping his hands behind his head and grinning evilly at me. "Yeah...but what would old Charlie say if I told him you had? And if I told him you came across as such an incompetent I could hardly believe it?"

"You wouldn't!" I whispered, although the expression on his face said he'd do it without a moment's hesitation.

What he said next was a real surprise, though. "You're right, I wouldn't."

I exhaled slowly, starting to relax.

But Rev put a quick stop to that by adding, "At least, I wouldn't call old Charlie about you so long as you agreed to let me work with you."

I STOOD STARING across Revington York's desk at him for what seemed like a year, trying to remember if I'd ever before grown to hate anyone so quickly and so intensely.

I decided I hadn't. Not in *this* lifetime, at least.

"So?" he said with an absolutely infuriating smile. "Partners?"

"Look, Mr. York—"

"Rev. I told you, call me Rev. And I'll call you Marina. Partners should be on first-name terms."

"Look, *Rev*," I snapped, almost choking on his name, "I'm not running the show here. I only got handed a bit part. For all I know, when I check in with Charlie, he'll tell me I'm off the case entirely."

"Then let's check in with him and see," Rev said, gesturing at his phone.

I gazed at it, starting to weigh my options, then realized I didn't have any. I certainly didn't intend to let this creep blackmail me, which meant I had to tell Charlie that Revington York was onto us. After Charlie had specifically told me to just see what I could learn *without* being obvious.

Of course, it was the blasted phone call from Rev's museum friend that had messed things up. And there wouldn't have been any phone call if Charlie had been more circumspect with his questions.

But Charlie was better at delegating blame than accepting it, so odds were it would end up squarely on my shoulders. And I was liable to find myself back in Auto Claims faster than I could say, "mummy case."

Unless... maybe Revington York was only bluffing. Surely a guy who was known as The Rev must have at least a little Christian charity in his soul. I glanced at him, wondering if I should call his bluff.

The minute I decided to try he shook his head. The man had to read minds on the side, because he said, "We're talking about my business being hurt the way things are going. So I wouldn't have a qualm about telling your Charlie whatever came into my head to say."

So much for Christian charity. I was caught between the proverbial rock and hard place. My all-time favorite position.

"I can't agree to your idea all on my own," I finally said, managing to sound at least halfway civil. "Working with someone outside the company would be highly irregular, so I'll have to run the idea by Charlie."

Rev didn't say a word, simply gestured toward the phone again.

"Do you have a number for the Donner?"

While he was flipping through his Rolodex I had another thought. When he scribbled down the phone number, I took the scrap of paper from him, saying, "I'm going to use the phone on your secretary's desk, okay? I have to make a quick personal call first. A good friend is in the hospital. You wouldn't have San Francisco General's number there, too, would you?"

He shook his head, eyeing me suspiciously, but said, "There's a telephone book in the bottom drawer of Rachel's desk."

There was a special number listed for patient rooms. I got through on the first try and asked the woman who answered for Nat Fishbein's room. I'd see how he was, and if he claimed to be as fine as Charlie had made out, I'd try asking for a little fatherly advice.

I couldn't risk getting Nat upset, of course, but I could try easing around the edges of this situation. Make a joke of it by telling him I'd been dealt a crazy suspect who wanted to play investigator with me. Explain I didn't know how I should approach Charlie about it and... well, I'd just have to see what advice I could get without saying anything that would cause even a blip in Nat's heartbeat.

"I'm sorry," the woman said, coming back on the line. "We aren't putting calls through to Mr. Fishbein's room."

I closed my eyes, afraid to ask how he was, then forced myself to.

"Stable condition," the woman said. "And he's not in critical care. But no phone calls and only family visitors. It's standard procedure for the first couple of days. I'm sure there's nothing to worry about," she added kindly. "And if you'd like, we can let him know you called."

I gave my name, thanked her and hung up, thinking I'd send Nat flowers. Tiger lilies, maybe. At least their name was masculine.

The fact that he was a long way from death's door made me feel good. His being incommunicado, though, made me feel anything but. I didn't know how on earth I should start things off with Charlie.

I glanced back toward Rev's office, relieved to see he was working at his desk, not paying any obvious attention to me. I could certainly do without him leaning over my shoulder.

Anxiously, I dialed the Donner's number and asked Security to locate Charlie for me.

By the time he picked up, I'd decided to take the bull by the horns and began by telling him about the phone call Revington York had gotten.

That started Charlie off on his bluster routine. "I've been asking questions about a *lot* of people," he snapped. "Revington York, yes. But also about everyone at the museum here who had anything to do with mounting the exhibit."

"Well . . . I just thought I should let you know. Because Rev was making noises about calling his lawyer . . . seemed to have the impression you'd been slandering him."

Charlie scoffed loud and long at that, assuring me there'd been nothing slanderous in anything he'd said. I didn't comment, but I knew that wasn't necessarily true. Nobody would ever accuse Charlie of subtlety.

"So," he finally said, "aside from that nonsense, your meeting went okay?"

"Well . . ." Here I was at show time and still without a script. There was nothing to do but plunge ahead and ad-lib. "Charlie, something happened I wasn't expecting. Revington York wants to tag along with me. Says he wants to help clear his name."

I held my breath through the long, ominous silence at the other end.

"Well, isn't that a surprising turn of events," Charlie said at last.

I began breathing again. He hadn't delivered the line I'd been dreading. The one about hustling myself back to Auto Claims.

"You know, Marina, there's always something to be said for getting close to a suspect. And if he's giving us a wide-open invitation, maybe we should take him up on it."

"Ahh . . . you're sure that's a good idea, Charlie?" I didn't think it was a good idea at all. Charlie was saying "us" and "we," but the only one of *us* who'd be doing any getting close was me. And I wasn't exactly crazy about the thought of getting close to a guy who might have . . . damn, but I wished I could stop thinking about that woman somebody had mummified.

"What's the matter?" Charlie said. "Don't you think you're up to playing along with him?"

"Of course I am," I lied, shoving my worries into a dark recess of my mind and telling them to stay there. If I had to work with Revington York, so be it. I'd figure out how to handle it.

"Good," Charlie was going on, "because this might turn out just fine. The next thing I was thinking you should do was talk to the Careful Wheels drivers. The ones who transported the exhibit up from L.A. And watch closely for their reactions. There should be some interesting interplay if their boss is with you.''

"Charlie? About L.A.," I said, his mention of it having jogged my memory. "What about the possibility that the real mummy case never left the museum there? That it was the reproduction they crated and shipped?''

"Yeah, that *is* a possibility. But I want to start with what happened after the exhibit was loaded onto the van. That's when Sherwin McNee's policy went into effect, remember?''

"Yes, but what if—''

"Marina, if the police find the switch was made before the case was shipped, great. We'll have no liability. But we have to focus on the period when our policy was covering the damned thing. I want that checked out first and fast.''

"But what if the police don't solve the case?" I asked really quickly, so Charlie couldn't interrupt my question a second time. "If they don't, and if the L.A. people keep insisting they crated the genuine article, then Sherwin McNee would end up having to make good on the claim, right?''

"Well . . . yes.''

Charlie often wasn't any better at accepting suggestions than he was at accepting blame, but I took a deep breath and risked pressing on. "Then don't you think we should be digging around at both ends? I mean, if there *was* something fishy going on in L.A., we'd only find out about it from someone there, right?''

There was another long silence while he considered my logic. I was positive he'd find a flaw somewhere, but he eventually said, "You *do* have a point.''

I felt like hugging myself. Charlie Obregon had said something complimentary about my investigating skills.

"Not that I think the switch *was* made in L.A.," he continued. "My money is still on Revington York. But I guess it would look better in my report if we cover both angles immediately. I can't waste *my* time running around the entire state, though. You'll have to go down."

"I'll have to go to L.A., you mean?" I said, afraid I had it wrong, that he wasn't really going to trust the job to me.

"What the hell else would I mean?" Charlie snapped. "Talk to those drivers today, then grab a flight to L.A. tomorrow. No point running up a hotel bill tonight when you don't have to."

"Right. I'll call the museum there and set up an appointment with that Egyptologist..."

"Professor Heinrich Reinhardt," Charlie supplied.

"Right. And I'll book the first flight in the morning."

"Good. Research can put together a file for you on what we know about how things were handled at that end. I'll have them courier it to your apartment."

"Great," I said, then hung up before Charlie could have second thoughts.

The urge to hug myself had grown twice as strong. Charlie was sending *me* to L.A. to check things out there. All alone!

I might have to put up with Revington York tagging along today, but I certainly wasn't letting him go with me to L.A. Charlie hadn't said a word about that, and there had to be limits to this getting close to the suspect routine. So I just wouldn't tell our suspect what I had on for tomorrow.

"So," Revington York said, practically into my ear. I wheeled around in the chair.

He was standing not more than a foot from me.

From my sitting position I was staring directly at his belt buckle—and the surrounding areas of his jeans and lower chest. It was most disconcerting.

Since the first moment I'd seen him, I'd been trying to ignore the fact that the man had the sort of build a lot of people work out long and hard to achieve. But ignoring it was difficult to do when my face was practically pressed against his body.

Quickly, I looked up. Ogling suspects was definitely not part of my job description.

His arms were folded across his broad chest, and he was wearing another of his infuriating smiles.

"So," he said again, "we're off to L.A. in the morning, are we?"

I started thinking about the little snub-nosed .38 in my bag. The idea of permanently getting rid of this six-foot-plus problem that had been foisted on me was awfully appealing. The idea of life imprisonment wasn't, though. I told myself to calm down and make the best of the situation.

"Your Charlie *did* agree to my idea, didn't he?" Rev persisted.

"He *kind of* agreed," I admitted. "But he didn't say anything about L.A. being part of *your* itinerary."

"No? Well, hell, let's just add it on. I've got the price of the airfare. We *are* flying, aren't we? You did say the first flight in the morning, didn't you?"

I could feel my teeth clenching. There was no way I could keep him off that plane and he knew it. The man was impossible. And I was stuck with him. But hadn't

I just finished telling myself to make the best of the situation?

I tried to smile. It was tough with clenched teeth.

"Look...Rev, for this arrangement to work, there have to be clear ground rules. *My* ground rules. And the basic one is that *I'm* in charge."

"Sounds fair," he said agreeably. "You're the detective."

I almost reminded him I was the insurance adjuster, but let it pass. He'd be more likely to go along with my calling the shots if he actually believed I knew what I was doing.

Not that I was sure he really had the slightest intention of letting me call the shots. My suspicious mind said he was merely humoring me. Revington York didn't strike me as the kind of man who did what *any- one* told him if he didn't want to.

"All right, then. Partners," I muttered unhappily.

The Rev's grin said we'd just become fast friends.

It sent an anxious shiver down my spine. Me be friends with a guy who might have done what he might have done? Not likely.

Chapter Three

I glanced across the car at Revington York as he drove, wondering how often people blackmailed their way into being someone's partner.

Nice guy, my temporary partner. A man with a heart as black as the ace of spades. And come tomorrow... damn, I didn't even want to think about that gruesome prospect. An entire round trip to Los Angeles with him for company. Bad enough being stuck with him today.

The drivers we were on our way to talk to, the ones who'd transported the museum exhibit from L.A. to the Donner, were working on a packing job near Fisherman's Wharf. Rev, though, hadn't bothered to mention the location until after we'd started off.

If he had, I'd never have agreed to his idea of taking only one car. His, naturally. He'd dismissed my old Mustang with a single contemptuous glance, then steered me to his shiny black Porsche. A shiny black 911 Porsche Carrera 2 Cabriolet, to be precise.

Between it and his condo that Research said was on Russian Hill, I'd started wondering if Charlie was wrong about Careful Wheels being in financial difficulty. There was no sign its owner was suffering.

I'd never even seen a Cabriolet before, but from my background in Auto Claims I knew it was worth close to a hundred thou, and I'd quickly begun to see why. I'd been in planes with less instrumentation, and the car was built to racing standards.

Rev's choice in cars seemed a little excessive, but didn't really surprise me. A few of the details Research had pulled together about him had told me he liked the finer things of life.

But at least the phone wasn't plugged in, which meant he wasn't one of those obsessive neurotics who can't stand to be unreachable for two minutes. I gave him credit for having *one* admirable attribute.

I did wonder, though, about the sanity of a man who'd choose to drive a standard shift up and down the hills of San Francisco.

At any rate, the problem with making the trip in *his* car was that my apartment in North Beach isn't far from Fisherman's Wharf. But now, instead of being able to go straight home after we saw his men, I'd have to drive all the way back to Careful Wheels, with him, to pick up my Mustang.

I couldn't help thinking that might be part of a plot he'd dreamed up to torture me, but decided I was being paranoid. I had an information file on him, not the other way around. He didn't know I lived in North Beach.

From here on in, though, there were going to be a lot more questions from me and a lot more answers from him before I'd agree to any of his suggestions.

Gazing out at the blur of buildings whizzing past on Van Ness, I did my best to ignore the speedometer and tried to think through the situation.

The way I saw it, there were two possible reasons Revington York was insisting on sticking his nose, along with the rest of him, where it didn't belong.

Number one was that he'd been telling me the truth. That he had nothing to do with the theft, but was afraid his company would be harmed if people started thinking he did.

I had to admit that the longer insurance people, not to mention the cops, wandered around asking questions about him, the more likely that scenario would become.

But the second possibility scared the hell out of me. If Revington York *had* been the brains behind the mummy-case switch, now he was trying to out-brain me.

At the very least, he figured putting on an act of trying to prove his innocence would throw me off track. And as a bonus, weaseling in on my investigation would let him see what I was doing and learn what I was finding out. Maybe he even had ideas about interfering if I started uncovering things he didn't want uncovered.

I looked over at him again. He was relaxing against the black leather upholstery, one hand on the wheel, the other resting on the stick shift.

He might be lean, but he looked strong. Broad shoulders and a chest that, from the way his shirt stretched across it, had to be muscular. He also had a good six inches in height on me.

I might have started self-defense classes, but I was a millenium away from a black belt. I tried to imagine how far he'd go if he decided that interfering was warranted. It's too bad I have a vivid imagination. It kept coming up with images of a mummified woman.

He turned left onto Chestnut, then took a right into an alley and parked behind a Careful Wheels moving van. That put us directly beside a sign that warned cars parked in the loading zone would be towed.

I got out of the Porsche, eyeing the loading dock unhappily as Rev hopped up onto it. Not much of a feat for a guy with long legs and wearing jeans. But for a woman in a straight skirt and heels, it would be a little trickier.

"Want a hand?" he said, looking back down and offering me one.

His expression was fifty percent grin, fifty percent leer, and one hundred percent annoying.

I *didn't* want a hand. Not his, at least. But I didn't have much choice.

He hauled me up easily, confirming my suspicion that he was strong. "Know thine enemy" might be good advice, but knowledge didn't always instill confidence.

Once I was on the dock, I brushed off what dust I could from the skirt of my white linen suit and followed him into the warehouse. Sure enough, two men in their thirties were busy packing antiques.

When Rev told them I was an insurance type, trying to establish what had happened to the mummy case, I watched carefully for the interesting interplay Charlie had predicted.

Neither of the men even glanced at their boss. Or at each other, for that matter.

"This is Bud, Marina," Rev went on, nodding at the taller man. "And Lou," he added, gesturing toward the shorter, chubby one.

Bud and Lou. As in Abbott and Costello? I looked at Rev, thinking this might be his idea of humor, but he didn't smile. What the hell. For all I knew, he had other guys named Groucho, Harpo and Chico.

Bud and Lou gave me exactly the same story about transporting the exhibit that Rev had. The crates had been loaded in L.A., then Bud and Lou had driven virtually nonstop to the Donner. Impossible, they insisted, that the switch was made while the mummy case was in their care.

Impossible, I thought, unless they were in on the caper. It would have taken no time at all for two men to have substituted one crate for another.

Even less time for *three* men, I amended my thought, glancing at Revington York. Two drivers and a man who'd brought the crated reproduction to a meeting place along their route. A place where they'd made the switch.

By the time Rev and I climbed back into his car, I was feeling darned discouraged. So far, I'd spent the entire day learning nothing useful.

If it wasn't going to be a total washout, I decided as he backed down the ally and out onto Chestnut, I'd better get him talking and hope he said something of interest.

"I guess that being in your business," I tried, "you must have learned a lot about art and antiques."

"A fair bit."

Obviously, I needed practice at getting a sparkling conversation going. I came up with another line and tried again. "You know, I've started wishing I knew more about Ancient Egypt. Reading the material Charlie gave me on the mummy case really got me interested."

"Yeah?" Rev glanced across at me. "I've got a few books you could borrow. And we're not far from my place. Want me to swing by?"

That was more like it. If he *was* our mastermind, a look around his apartment might reveal something useful. "Sure, that would be great," I said.

He took a left and a couple of minutes later we were winding our way up Russian Hill, past its variety of housing—different-hued single-family homes, Victorian flats and pricey condos.

Rev's condo was in a modern three-story brick building with spacious balconies and wraparound windows. Fleetingly, I wondered how safe they'd be in an earthquake, then I focused on the brass double doors of the main entrance. They shone as if someone polished them daily.

"Coming in?" Rev said.

I nodded and followed him out of the car and into the building. We bypassed the elevator and walked up to the third floor, but his apartment was definitely not what anyone would refer to as a "walk-up."

Instead of a standard tiny entrance hall, it had an elegant foyer paneled in smoked glass. The floor was pale marble tile, and there was enough room for an antique hall table that displayed several small art objects.

Before I had a chance to look at them closely, Rev was leading the way into the living room, casually tossing his keys on the table as he walked past.

Unlike his minimal beige office, his living room had an eclectic combination of antiques and the kind of overstuffed furniture that makes you want to sink into it and never get up again.

The creamy marble floor continued in from the foyer; the walls were chocolate brown; the furniture a combination of the two colors. Through the wraparound window, I could see the bay in the distance.

"This is gorgeous," I said. "Who did your decorating?"

"I did. I'll just get those books. They're in the den."

I stood gazing around, taking in more details. I hadn't suspected Revington York of having such good taste. Then I spotted something else I wouldn't have suspected.

In one corner of the living room, beside an enormous leather chair I'd bet was his favorite, a gilt bird cage hung from a stand. Inside the cage, peering over at me, was a canary.

Rev was just full of surprises. If a rotter like him had mentioned having a bird, I'd have assumed it was a vulture.

I wandered across for a closer look, and the canary gave a few excited chirps. In addition to water and birdseed, there was a little plate that held pecked-at slivers of apple and orange. I tried to imagine Revington York chopping away at tiny bits of fruit every morning.

Before I got my imagination up to speed he reappeared, a couple of books in his hand, saying, "I haven't read these for years. But from what I remember, they were pretty interesting."

"Thanks. They'll give me something to read tonight. What's your friend's name?" I added, glancing at the bird again.

Rev mumbled something I didn't catch.

"Pardon?" I said, turning back.

"Tweetie," he repeated a touch more clearly.

He looked so embarrassed it was all I could do not to laugh.

"I'm *not* responsible for the name," he said defensively. "Tweetie used to belong to my next-door neighbor. She named him."

"And then gave him to you?"

"She had to go into a nursing home last year. And when she asked me to take the bird I had no choice. It was like a damned kid to her. Every time I go to visit her, he's the first thing she asks about."

"Oh," I said, mentally giving Rev credit for a second admirable attribute. It wasn't nearly enough to move him out of the rotter category, but maybe his heart wasn't *quite* as black as the ace of spades.

It still might be, of course. Just because he had a soft spot for an old lady and was good to a bird . . . well, the Birdman of Alcatraz had been good to birds and I was pretty sure he was a murderer. Killers were almost the only people who got sent to Alcatraz.

We started for the door, but one of the things on the foyer table caught my eye as Rev picked up his keys.

"Mummy beads," he said, his eyes following my gaze.

"Pardon?"

"It's the sort of necklace you'd find on a mummy."

"Really?" I said, my mind racing. What on earth were mummy beads doing in his apartment?

"You mean it's the kind of necklace Princess Amonit would have been wearing?" I ventured, watching closely for his reaction.

There wasn't a noticeable one. He simply said, "Right. But hers would have been authentic. Those are from the gift shop at the Donner. They're selling various reproductions of Egyptian artifacts while the exhibit is on. Somebody in PR sent those over to the office for me."

"Oh?" I said. If he was lying, he was a darned good liar. But that would be in character with being a manipulative, blackmailing rotter.

"Yeah," he said. "They arrived just after we delivered the exhibit pieces. Came with a note thanking me for a job well done. Ironic, huh? I get accolades from the museum. Then, next thing I hear, your boss is running all over it calling me a crook."

I picked up the beads, wishing I knew something about old Egyptian jewelry.

There were six strands, each strung in the same pattern of navy, red and turquoise beads. I assumed these ones were glass, but had no idea what would have been used in the original necklace.

"These aren't real gold, are they?" I asked, fingering the three charms that hung from the bottom strand.

Rev shrugged. "I doubt it. If the necklace was genuine, though, they'd be electrum—a mixture of gold and silver the Egyptians used."

Fascinated by their designs, I turned one of the charms over.

"A fish amulet," Rev said. "It was to prevent drowning."

"And this one?" I asked, resting the small golden shell in my hand.

He smiled at me. "You really *have* gotten interested in Egyptian stuff, haven't you? That's a cowrie shell. It shows the wearer wanted to have children."

Absently, I wondered if Princess Amonit had been a mother.

"And the one in the middle is Heh," Rev said. "He's the god who symbolizes long life."

"You're really up on your Egyptian history."

"No, I'm actually pretty rusty. I just looked up what those charms represented after the beads arrived."

I glanced back at the little image of Heh. He was a delicate fellow, kneeling in a sideways position but facing straight at me. Looking at him gave me the strangest urge to put the necklace on.

"Try it on," Rev said.

The suggestion sent an anxious feeling racing through me. Earlier, when I'd decided to call his bluff about blackmailing me, Rev had displayed a similar mind-reading ability. I found it darned unsettling.

Regardless of that, though, I fastened the beads around my neck and gazed at them in the smoky mirrored paneling of the foyer.

"You like them?" Rev asked.

"They're beautiful."

"Keep them, then. They look great on you."

"Oh, no, I couldn't," I said, looking at him in the mirror.

"No, really," he persisted. "The museum's sending them to me was a nice gesture, but I'm not into wearing women's jewelry."

"No, thank you, but I couldn't." Reluctantly, I reached to unfasten them.

"Marina, keep them. What am I going to do with fake mummy beads? I offered them to my secretary when they arrived at the office, but she said they looked like junk."

His secretary had to have rocks in her head. The beads were wonderful.

You're not supposed to take a gift from a suspect...but I couldn't resist. "Well, if you're really sure..."

"I'm really sure," he said, smiling at me again. "But speaking of my secretary, we'd better get going. I've got to check my machine for messages and leave a note on Rachel's desk for tomorrow. She said she'd make it in whether she was still feeling rotten or not, so the least I should do is let her know what's happening."

I nodded, realizing that for a minute *I'd* been forgetting about what was happening.

Well, to be honest, Revington York had turned on the charm and *made* me forget. That smile of his was disarming. Alarmingly disarming, considering the situation. I'd have to be a darned sight more careful about not letting down my guard around him.

Tall, dark and charming might be a terrific combination in a regular guy, but in a prime suspect it was dangerous as hell.

ON THE WAY HOME from Careful Wheels my trusty Mustang had uncharacteristically coughed a few times. So, in the morning, I opted for a taxi to San Francisco International. I wasn't taking any chances on blowing the first real assignment Charlie had given me.

There wasn't any sign of Rev in the terminal, and by the time I picked up my ticket and boarding pass the flight was being called. That really got my hopes up. Then he dashed them by materializing at my side.

He was wearing a grey pin-striped suit, a crisp white shirt, and not more than a four-o'clock shadow. He looked downright civilized, even with his too-long hair.

I wasn't fooled, though. It took more than an expensively tailored suit to conceal the dark and dangerous aura I'd sensed yesterday.

Even if he could transform himself into looking as if he was on his way to an appointment with his banker, I was sure yesterday's somewhat uncivilized man in jeans was the real Revington York. That hard-edged, take-charge masculinity was unmistakable... and unnerving.

"Hey," he said, grinning at me, "those really do look great."

Self-consciously, I fingered the mummy beads. I'd hesitated a long time about wearing them, but they *did* look nice. Their colors set off my pale blue suit perfectly.

"I was reading your books last night," I explained. "And somehow it just felt right to put these on this morning."

Our flight was being called for the second time, so we headed to the departure lounge.

Having picked up our tickets separately, we didn't have seats together on the plane. That meant I was free to spend the short trip with my nose buried in the most recent file Research had compiled.

I'd looked through it late yesterday, when it had arrived at my apartment, and I didn't pick up anything more from it the second time through. It didn't take an expert on museum procedures to realize that moving the exhibit had been handled in a logical manner.

Ashton Crawly, exhibition coordinator at the Donner, had gone to L.A. several months ago. He'd conferred with Professor Heinrich Reinhardt, Chief Egyptologist at the museum there, and together they'd selected the pieces that would be put on display in San Francisco.

Then, once the exhibit space had been readied at the Donner, Reinhardt had supervised the removal of the pieces from display in his museum and had his people crate them for shipping. What could have been more straightforward than that?

Of course, the whole point of this trip was to make sure everything actually *had* been as straightforward as it appeared on the surface, and that the forgery hadn't been substituted before the exhibit left L.A. Given the information in the file, it seemed that there were only two people at the L.A. museum who could possibly have taken part in the hypothetical switch.

The first was Professor Reinhardt. The second was a man named Mickey Flynn, head of the L.A. museum's shipping and receiving department. He'd been responsible for crating the exhibit pieces.

When I'd set up our appointment with Professor Reinhardt, he'd assured me we'd be able to talk to the people in shipping as well.

Once the plane landed, Rev and I made our way into the zoo that was LAX. I started for the nearest taxi stand. Rev, though, had a different idea.

"Come on," he said, pointing to where the airport limos were waiting. "Morning rush hour isn't over, so the ride could take forever. We might as well be comfortable." He turned and headed through the crowd without waiting for a reply.

I started after him, telling myself that the minute we were on our way into town I'd remind him he'd agreed to play by *my* rules.

Once inside the limo, though, I was distracted by a discreet little card that announced the fare to downtown. If it had been posted outside, I'd have insisted on a taxi. Or maybe even a bus.

By the time I'd gotten over the price shock, Rev had flicked on the television and was engrossed in a news program.

After a moment's thought, I decided to hold back on reminding him that I was supposed to be running the show. It would hardly help our cause to be at each other's throat when we met Professor Reinhardt.

So instead of confronting Revington York, I spent the entire hour in the limo worrying about how I was going to justify the cost of our ground transportation to Charlie.

When we arrived at the museum I charged the trip, making myself add on a reasonable tip. Maybe, by the time the bill arrived, the real mummy case would have been recovered. Then Charlie might be in an understanding mood.

Thanks to the traffic, we were almost half an hour late for our appointment with Professor Reinhardt. He rose behind his desk when his secretary led us into his office, but greeted us with a frown rather than the standard pleasantries.

One of the lenses in his glasses was cracked, and the way he was fiddling with them made me think it had just happened. I apologized for being late, but his frown remained. Then his expression suddenly changed to a startled one when he noticed my necklace.

"Where did you get that?" he demanded, obviously as given to subtlety as Charlie Obregon. He squinted through his cracked glasses at it, then took them off and continued looking at the necklace. "Whole damned world's blurry today," he muttered.

"It's something they're selling in the Donner's gift shop," I explained. "It's a copy of—"

"I know what it's a copy of," he interrupted, dropping back into his chair and waving us into the visitors' ones. "I'm not entirely blind with this lens broken. Just can't see detail. I can make out that it's a copy of Princess Amonit's necklace, though. But I didn't know they were having reproductions of it made. It wasn't one of the items Ashton Crawly and I discussed as a possibility. They must have used one of our mummy X rays to get the design.''

The Professor clearly wasn't pleased that the necklace had been copied. And he clearly wasn't pleased to be entertaining Rev and me, either. He sat glaring across his desk at us.

Professor Reinhardt was about sixty, a touch taller than average, and carried forty or fifty extra pounds, which made him distinctly pear-shaped.

What was left of his hair was a mousy brown, and his graying eyebrows rose bushily behind the wire-rimmed glasses. He was wearing an ancient tweed suit with matching vest and, believe it or not, an old-fashioned pocket watch on a chain.

Surreptitiously, I let my gaze wander across the neat surface of his desk, looking for a meerschaum pipe. It would have completed the picture perfectly, and I was disappointed not to see one.

When I looked back up, the Professor was staring straight at me. ''Have we met before?'' he demanded.

''Ahh . . . no, I'm sure I'd remember if we had.''

''Strange,'' he muttered. ''There's something terribly familiar about your face.''

I swallowed uneasily, recalling how peculiar I'd felt when I'd first seen that photograph of Princess Amonit's painted face. Had Professor Reinhardt picked up on the similarity between our looks?

While I was mentally debating whether or not to mention it, the Professor took his watch out of its little pocket in his vest and pointedly looked at it.

That made me decide to get right down to business, so I apologized again for keeping him waiting, then basically repeated what I'd told him when I'd called yesterday.

"So," I concluded, "if you wouldn't mind just physically walking us through what happened to the pieces, from the time they were removed from their permanent display until they were loaded onto the Careful Wheels van..."

"Yes, yes," he muttered, "it's all arranged. But I told the head of shipping that we'd be there by now. Do you care if I show you everything in the exact order it happened? Mickey Flynn is a rather impatient man."

That seemed to be a common trait here. Maybe there was something in the air that caused it, something about the infamous L.A. smog. But I doubted it would be wise to ask, so I merely told the Professor I didn't think it would matter if we went to shipping first.

I barely finished getting the words out before we were on our way there.

Mickey Flynn turned out not only to be impatient but also extremely uneasy about Revington and me asking questions. He clearly took them as an affront to his honesty.

"I *personally* supervised the crating," he finally snapped. "Everything gets sealed so nobody can mess with stuff after that. There weren't any forgeries in those crates."

"But we're talking about an excellent forgery," I pointed out. "Nobody at the Donner realized there'd been a switch until Professor Reinhardt arrived. So couldn't you possibly have crated the substitute thinking it was the real thing?"

Mickey Flynn looked at the Professor, but I couldn't decipher the glance that passed between them. I wondered if Nat Fishbein would have been able to, and longed once again for his thirty years of experience.

"Two of my men," Mickey said, turning back to me, "got the stuff Professor Reinhardt told them to get from the displays. And I made sure it got crated right. Okay?"

I looked at Rev.

He shook his head. Mickey Flynn had told his story. More questions would be superfluous.

"Well, then," the Professor said, "why don't I take you to the Egyptian Gallery?"

We'd barely left the shipping department when Professor Reinhardt's secretary appeared to tell him he had an important phone call.

"Can I get you anything?" the woman asked as he bustled off. "Coffee?"

"No, thanks," Rev said before I could answer.

I was dying for a coffee. I *should* have straightened out who was in charge back in the limo.

"I know Tony Vespucci in Administration," Rev was telling the secretary. "So I think I'll stick my head into his office, if you wouldn't mind letting Professor Reinhardt know where we'll be."

Tony Vespucci, Rev explained as we started off on our own, was the fellow who looked after the administrative side of tasks like loaning out exhibits. "I've dealt with him a few times," he added, "and he's a regular guy. Maybe he can give us the real goods on Reinhardt."

"The real goods?" I said. Reading the file material, the Professor had seemed an obvious suspect. But now that I'd met him, I doubted he had anything to do with what had happened.

"Yeah," Rev said, "you can tell Reinhardt's weird just by looking at him."

Before I could ask exactly what Rev's definition of weird entailed, we reached Tony Vespucci's office and Rev was introducing me.

Tony was only about Rev's age, but the photograph on his desk showed him with a wife and four kids.

"You don't really think anyone at this end was involved, do you?" he asked when Rev explained what we were up to.

"Who knows?" Rev said. "But what about this Professor Reinhardt? What's the scoop on him?"

"The Rhino?" Tony said, grinning. "Hell, he's the last guy in the world who'd have been in on a switch. I heard he just about went into cardiac arrest at the Donner, when he realized someone had stolen the mummy case. It wasn't really ours, you know. It's owned privately—some rich guy who lives in La Jolla lent it to us years ago."

I nodded. I'd remembered that from the Research file.

"Anyway," Tony went on, "I think its not being ours made the Rhino feel even worse about losing it. But he's a fanatic about the entire collection. You'd figure everything in Egyptology belonged to *him,* rather than to the museum."

"Yeah, we already had him pegged as kind of weird," Rev said.

Tony laughed. "I'll have to admit a lot of people say he is. A few of them even say The Rhino has a private art collection in a secret room in his house. You wonder how rumors like that get started."

I thought of Nat Fishbein again, of those stories he'd told me about wealthy private art collectors who had no ethical problems with buying hot works of art or artifacts. And I couldn't help wondering if there were private collectors who weren't wealthy, but who had opportunities to steal, rather than buy.

Chapter Four

"And this, of course, is *my* gallery," Professor Reinhardt said, waving his hand peremptorily when we reached the entrance to the Egyptian wing.

Just as Tony Vespucci had remarked, you'd think it belonged to the Professor, rather than to the museum. But would he really have stolen the mummy case so he could keep it in a secret room in his house?

Absurd as that idea seemed to me, there were a lot of weird people in the world. And I was dying to ask why Rev was so certain the Professor was one of them.

I'd give him that Reinhardt was unusual. Maybe even eccentric, if today's old-fashioned suit was his standard style of dress. But, to my mind, weird meant distinctly warped.

Before I'd had a chance to talk to Rev alone, though, Reinhardt had come by Tony's office and collected us.

"You could spend days here," the Professor said, starting us down the gallery's long center aisle. "So I'll only be able to point out a highlight or two."

I followed along with Rev, trying to work my way through the Heinrich Reinhardt puzzle systematically, the way Nat Fishbein had taught me. Focus on opportunity and motive. That was Nat's rule.

All right. The Professor could easily have had a fake mummy case made. He certainly knew people capable of doing that. And, one way or another, he could have replaced the authentic one with the fake before Mickey Flynn crated it. Or Flynn could have been involved. And if Reinhardt really *was* a private collector, that would cover motive.

Everything was speculation, though. Speculation based on rumor.

And wasn't it kind of strange that Tony Vespucci would mention that rumor in front of me? A complete stranger? *And* someone who worked for Sherwin McNee Indemnity?

The more I thought about that, the more peculiar I found it.

I glanced at Rev. He *had* to know I shared Charlie's suspicions about him. So how far would he go to deflect my suspicions away from him and onto somebody like Heinrich Reinhardt?

As far as having staged that conversation with Tony for my benefit?

For all I knew, the rumor was something Revington York had cooked up. He could easily have phoned Tony yesterday and gotten his cooperation.

Mr. Revington York was *not* to be trusted, I reminded myself. His sole interest in this was clearing his name, whether it deserved to be cleared or not. So, it could be that the rumor about the Professor having a private art collection was a brainchild of my prime suspect.

"Look at this," Reinhardt ordered, stopping in front of a huge glass case containing a replica of an Egyptian tomb. The stone walls and ceiling were entirely covered with paintings.

"Some of those are scenes from daily living," he explained, "to make the mummy feel at home. The others depict passage into the afterlife. And the items entombed with the mummy were all things that would aid the *ka*, as the Egyptians called the soul, during its passage."

I gazed at the tomb full of artifacts. The focal point of the display was a heavily carved stone sarcophagus, surrounded by both treasures and everyday items.

From the books Rev had lent me, I knew the bowls and goblets would have held food and drink for the soul's voyage. The *ka's* voyage, I mentally corrected myself.

And the small boat was there in case it encountered water on its trip. The jewelry was to ensure that souls already in the afterlife recognized the newcomer as a person of importance.

Absently, I brushed my hand across my mummy beads, wondering what the original ones would have indicated about Princess Amonit.

"What does that say?" Rev asked, pointing to the stone door that stood open on one side of the tomb. There was something written on it in hieroglyphics.

"It's a curse," Heinrich Reinhardt said. "It threatens dire consequences to anyone who disturbs the mummy."

"Curses on tombs were pretty common, weren't they," Rev said.

The Professor nodded. "They were meant to deter thieves from stealing the treasures, by playing on common beliefs about the spirit world. According to Egyptian myth, there were two forms to the soul. The one I mentioned, the *ka*, eventually traveled to the afterlife. But the other, the *ba*, could come and go through the walls of the tomb forever to protect the mummy... or seek revenge, as the case might be."

"I was reading about that last night," I offered.

The comment earned me a nod of approval from Professor Reinhardt.

I decided not to add that my reading had led to a nightmare, full of mummies wakening from the dead and *ba*s flying around.

"And just down at the end of the gallery," Reinhardt said, starting off again, "is the exhibit that featured the mummy case. In fact, many of the pieces we sent to the Donner came from that display."

We stopped in front of a floor-to-ceiling glass exhibit case that stretched the entire length of a wall. There were still pieces of furniture and artifacts inside, but interspersed among them were numerous placards, stating that the item normally there was on loan to another museum.

"That's where the mummy case rested," the Professor said, pointing to a placard in the center of the display.

"So... is there anything else you need to see?" he added after a minute.

I gazed at the place the mummy case belonged for another few seconds, then shook my head, wondering why I'd thought it was so important to see this. It was nothing more than an empty space in a giant display cabinet.

"Then, if we're done," Reinhardt said, "I'll leave you and get back to my office. And, Ms. Haine, I *do* hope you're successful. It would be tragic for the world to lose something as precious as the mummy case."

"I hope we're successful, too," I said. "Or that the police are. And thank you for your help. We really appreciate your taking the time to..." I paused, my peripheral vision catching a movement.

I looked back at the display case. For a long moment, I could see what was moving inside. And I knew it saw me. Something icy slithered up my spine as I watched it.

Then it darted sideways.

Just as it was vanishing behind a large statue, Rev said, "What the hell's that?"

A quick glance told me he'd seen the thing, too.

By the time I glanced back, it had disappeared. But I was left with with an incredibly eerie fluttering sensation, as if its tiny wings were beating inside me.

I stood staring at the statue it had flown behind, my heart pounding with the fear of confronting the inexplicable. I didn't believe in that sort of thing...yet I knew what I'd seen.

When I anxiously glanced at Rev again, he was gazing at me with an expression of total uncertainty.

"What's the problem?" Reinhardt demanded, looking from one of us to the other.

"It..." I waved my hand toward the case, part of me hoping the thing was gone forever, part of me hoping it would reappear so the Professor would see it. But all was motionless behind the glass.

"I saw a bird," I said at last. "Flying in there."

"No," he said. "You couldn't have. That case hasn't been opened in over a month. Not since the pieces were removed for shipping."

"But I *saw* it," I insisted, feeling idiotic because my brain was telling me I couldn't have. "I even saw where it went. It's behind that statue. Do you think..."

I paused and took a deep breath, not at all certain I wanted to ask the question.

"Do I think what?" the Professor asked.

"Would it be possible to open the case and check?"

He shook his head firmly. "We don't open a case unless it's essential. They're all climatically controlled and hermetically sealed."

"Look," Rev said, "I saw something in there, too."

Reinhardt shrugged. "I suppose it's possible. Occasionally, a bird does get into the museum."

"But how would it get inside the case?" I asked. "It was definitely on the other side of the glass."

"I'm an Egyptologist, not an ornithologist," the Professor said, his expression patronizing. "What do I know about bird behavior? But if it got in, I'm sure it can get out again. Now, if we *are* finished . . . ?"

For a moment, I considered telling Reinhardt what I'd *really* seen, then decided against it. He hadn't even caught a glimpse of the thing. And when he'd mentioned the *ka* and *ba* he'd said, "According to Egyptian *myth*."

In other words, they weren't beliefs *he* subscribed to. So if I pressed further, he'd figure I was a hysterical female.

"Yes, I guess we're finished," I finally said. "And thank you again. You don't mind if we stay and look around the gallery a little?"

"Not at all." Heinrich Reinhardt gave us a curt nod, then started back the way we'd come.

The minute he was out of hearing range, Rev said, "What the hell was it?"

"How good a look did you get at it?"

"Not good at all. There was just a flash of gray. Then it was gone."

I swore silently. If I told him exactly what *I'd* seen, he was going to decide I was crazy.

"I thought maybe it was a bat," he said.

"No. I'm sure it was a bird...kind of a bird, at least."

"What do you mean, kind of?"

"Well...it looked like a little gray bird...no bigger than a wren."

"Yeah, I guess that's what it must have been. Reinhardt did say birds occasionally get in."

"He said into the building, not into the cases. They're hermetically sealed. You heard him. There's something really freaky going on here."

"Hey, take it easy, Marina. It was only a bird. And no matter how well the case is sealed, it could have gotten in there while they were removing the pieces to send to the Donner."

"Over a month ago? It couldn't have lived that long with no food or water." I hesitated, then decided to take the plunge. "And, Rev...it was looking straight at me for a minute. It just hovered like a humming bird and stared right at me. And I got the spookiest feeling."

"Hey, sometimes Tweetie's stare seems kind of spooky. It's those beady little eyes birds have."

I shook my head. Now that I'd gone this far, there was no point in not laying it all on him. "It didn't look exactly like a normal bird," I made myself say.

"No? Then what exactly did it look like?"

"It's head wasn't right, Rev. Not for a bird. It looked like a tiny human head."

I WAITED AN ETERNITY, hoping Rev's knowledge of ancient Egypt wasn't as rusty as he'd made out yesterday, hoping he'd realize the significance of the tiny human head.

The more I had to explain, the crazier I was going to sound. And the way he was staring at me said he already figured I'd taken leave of my senses.

Finally I pressed on. Whether he figured I was losing it or not, this was far too bizarre for me to puzzle through on my own.

"Rev, all those things the ancient Egyptians believed in. Do you think there could be anything *to* any of them? Like their belief in the *ka*... and the *ba?*"

He shrugged. "Why not? They were just names for the soul. And even today, most people still believe in souls and an afterlife."

I stood gazing through the glass of the exhibit case, trying to get everything straight in my head, but I was certain I had the details about the *ba* right.

"What are you thinking?" Rev asked.

I continued to hesitate, feeling ridiculous. But no matter how strongly I reminded myself that I don't really believe in oogly-boogly stuff, I *had* seen that thing.

"Well?" Rev pressed.

"I...I'm thinking about something I read last night. And about what Reinhardt said. That there are two forms to the soul. That the *ka* eventually goes to the afterlife but the *ba* can come and go...and it protects the mummy."

"And?"

"And those books of yours said the Egyptians believed that when the *ba* does come and go... Rev, they believed that when it did it took the shape of a small bird. A bird with a human head resembling the dead person's."

Simply saying that out loud made me cringe inside. And the way Revington York was staring at me almost made me cringe outside as well.

He was trying to conceal what he was thinking. But I knew he was deciding whether or not to call for the men wearing white coats and carrying butterfly nets.

"I see," he said at last, slowly rubbing his jaw. "And this human-looking head you thought you saw...?"

I let his use of the word *thought* pass. Considering that I was the one who'd seen it, and *I* found it inconceivable, it was hardly surprising Rev did.

"You thought the bird you saw looked like Princess Amonit, right?"

I merely nodded. This definitely wasn't the time to mention it resembled *me*, as well.

"I see," Rev said a second time.

"*What* do you see?" I demanded.

"Well...I guess I see a problem with all this."

I waited for him to elaborate. I saw a problem with it all, too. Either I was loosing my marbles or we had entered the realm of the paranormal. And neither possibility thrilled me even a little bit.

Revington continued to rub his jaw thoughtfully for so long he was at risk of rubbing off his skin.

"Let's assume," he said at last, "that the Egyptians were right about there being an afterlife. Hell, let's even assume they had this *ka* and *ba* thing figured right. The problem I'm left with is that Princess Amonit died more than three thousand years ago. So I can't see how either her *ka* or *ba* could still be lurking around today."

"Professor Reinhardt said *forever*, remember? He said the *ba* could go back and forth through the walls of the tomb and protect the mummy *forever*." I couldn't help glancing at the display case as I spoke.

Rev's gaze followed mine. "And you figure," he said slowly, "that a hermetically sealed glass case is the equivalent of a tomb... at least, when it comes to going back and forth through walls?"

I nodded again, but my brain was beginning to hurt. And with each passing minute I was having more of a problem believing that Rev and I were standing here, two intelligent people, logically discussing something completely illogical. Yet, for some inexplicable reason, I couldn't just let the subject drop.

"What if," I asked, "there *is* something to this supernatural stuff? And something to that curse Reinhardt talked about? He said it was aimed at anyone who *disturbed* the mummy. And somebody *stole* Princess Amonit. That's about as disturbing as things could get for her. But to do anything to protect her, or get revenge or whatever, her *ba* would have to find her first."

"Marina... do you *really* believe that was Princess Amonit's *ba* we saw? Flying around searching for the stolen mummy?"

I closed my eyes. When he said it like that it sounded totally ludicrous.

"That's not," I murmured, "what I *really* believe. I mean, I don't really believe it could have been some sort of spirit. Not rationally I don't. It's just that there's the odd irrational thought I can't seem to ignore."

"But the only *reasonable* explanation is that, somehow, a bird got into that case. An ordinary bird. With an ordinary head. Somehow, your imagination made you see a human head... that's all."

His theory was something I had to consider. Especially when the idea of a three-thousand-year-old soul flying around like a bird went against everything I'd ever thought possible.

And I *did* have a vivid imagination. And I *had* spent last night immersed in those books, soaking up all their talk of *ka*s and *ba*s and a million other things that were great imagination triggers.

"So, Marina?"

"So... I guess you're right. I guess that's the only reasonable explanation. My mind must have been playing tricks."

Rev smiled, obviously relieved that he wouldn't get stuck having to check me into a rubber room someplace.

"Let's get out of here," he said. "You want to grab a late lunch at the airport or try to find a place around here?"

I told him the airport would be fine. I'm not a devotee of cardboard food, but the excitement had left me with a queasy feeling in my stomach that wasn't going to let me do justice to *any* food.

Silently, we started for the exit while I tried to convince myself my eyes really *had* been playing tricks on me.

I couldn't quite manage it, though. The bottom line was that nothing should have been alive in that case, but something had been. And I'd had an awfully good look at it, and I have twenty-twenty vision.

Surely there was a *better* reasonable explanation for what I'd seen than that my imagination had been working overtime. But damned if I could figure out what it might be.

FORTUNATELY AIRPORT LIMOS don't cruise Second Street. Which meant there was no option but a relatively inexpensive taxi to take us from the museum back to LAX.

And that meant I didn't have to get into a big deal with Revington York about my being the one in charge.

A major relief, considering that until I began to recover from my brush with the preternatural, I probably couldn't have managed being in charge of us crossing the street.

All I did for the first part of the ride was unsuccessfully try to make sense of what I'd seen in that exhibit case.

I don't know what Rev was thinking about, but he didn't say a word until we hit the Santa Monica Freeway. Then he asked what my impressions were of Heinrich Reinhardt and Mickey Flynn.

I looked at him blankly for a minute before I realized what he was getting at. The whole point of this trip had been to check out those two.

"Well," I said at last, "I got the feeling we can forget about Mickey Flynn. He didn't seem very bright, so I doubt he'd have initiated the plan. And if the Professor was behind it, he'd have kept the number of people involved to a minimum. Just himself and whoever created the forgery. They could probably have managed the switch before the case ever got to Flynn for crating."

"Which means you think it might have been Reinhardt?"

"No...not really." I wasn't quite sure what I thought, but nothing the Professor had said had set off any serious alarms in my head.

"I just don't know," I finally added. "*You* were the one who said he was weird. But you didn't tell me what made you think so."

"Marina, any guy who dresses in a heavy old tweed suit, in L.A., in July, is *definitely* weird."

"What? That's all you were going on? The way the man was dressed? Dressing funny isn't what I call *weird*, Rev."

"That wasn't *all*," he said defensively. "His crazy old suit and vest just really struck me. If they were ever in style it was a century ago. And the old watch and everything. And then there was what Tony Vespucci said. About that rumor."

"Right...that rumor." The rumor I'd suspected Revington York of having cooked up himself.

"Didn't you think it was kind of odd," I asked, eyeing him closely, "that Tony mentioned it in front of me? When he knew I was an insurance adjuster?"

Rev shrugged. "I guess he figured if you were a friend of mine you were all right."

I didn't bother pointing out that we were hardly friends. Instead, I merely said, "You think the Professor *might* have an art collection hidden away?"

"Who knows? And there's no way you and I could find out, short of breaking into his house and searching for a secret room. But you or your boss should probably mention it to the police, in case nobody else has. They might figure it's at least worth checking out."

I nodded slowly. Rev couldn't be accused of really playing up this angle, so maybe it hadn't been his invention, after all.

"The idea of old Reinhardt as a criminal, though," he went on, "well, my gut feeling says he didn't have a thing to do with what happened."

That was my gut feeling, too. And if we were right, it meant the switch had been made after the genuine mummy case had reached the Donner.

Either then, or while it was in Revington York's moving van.

Chapter Five

The plane to San Francisco was full, so Rev and I didn't end up sitting together on the flight home, either. I found my persistent wish that we *were* disconcerting.

After all, we'd pretty well written off both Professor Reinhardt and Mickey Flynn as suspects, which left Revington York's name precisely where it had started: smack at the top of Charlie's list.

And I wasn't even sure exactly what we should be suspecting Rev of. It was very possible our modern-day mummy was a murder victim. And whoever was responsible for the phony mummy case had to be responsible for the phony mummy, as well.

I certainly wished the results of that autopsy would come in. If she hadn't been murdered, I could relax on that score, at least. But, either way, my intuition had started saying Revington York wasn't a crook, let alone a murderer.

"So, you've got your car here?" Rev asked when we landed.

"No, I took a taxi this morning."

"Then I'll give you a ride."

There he went, taking charge again, but I barely cared. It's a fair distance from San Francisco International into the city, and I didn't want to be alone with my thoughts for another minute.

"What area do you live in?" he asked as we reached his Porsche.

When I told him North Beach he grinned, saying, "We're practically neighbors, then. You should have called me this morning, instead of a cab company."

Our timing was absolutely perfect for putting us in the middle of the afternoon rush hour. Even heading north into town, against most of the traffic, it was a long, slow trip.

Rev didn't say anything, but I suspected having to dawdle along below the speed limit was driving him crazy. The way he'd zoomed around town yesterday had told me he normally drove fast. Not surprising, given his car could do zero to sixty in six seconds.

"Hey," he said, glancing over when we passed the turnoff to San Jose. "Do you want to have an early dinner before we call it a day? That snack we grabbed at LAX just whetted my appetite, and there's a great little Mexican restaurant only a block from my place."

I gazed at him for a moment, wondering how differently I'd feel about that invitation if there wasn't a cloud of suspicion hanging over him.

He might not be exactly my type, and he *could* be infuriating, but there was no denying the man was...well, in one word, a hunk. The more I saw of him, the more I thought those photos in the Research file didn't do him justice.

And I really didn't believe there was even a chance he was a murderer. But regardless of how remote the possibility...

Besides, there was leftover chicken in my fridge that didn't have another day or two before mold set in.

"So?" he said. "Mexican? Or, there's a good pizza place that delivers."

"Mexican." The word just popped out, even though I'd been on the verge of saying no to either option.

I knew it was the idea of having something delivered to his apartment that had caused my choice.

I might not really believe he could be a murderer. And I might have a gun in my bag. But something told me that spending much time alone with Revington York, in his apartment, could be dangerous as hell.

"This restaurant," I said after we'd driven a few more miles. "It isn't too classy, is it? I'm feeling a little grubby."

He glanced over, saying, "You don't look grubby. But, no, the restaurant isn't classy. In fact, I'm going to stop by my apartment and change. I hate wearing suits."

When we reached his building, he wheeled into the underground lot beneath it, instead of pulling one of the illegal parking jobs I'd decided were his norm.

"Come on up," he said. "We'll leave the car here and walk to Casa del Sol. There isn't always a place to park any closer."

"I'll just be a minute," he said when we reached his door. "The main bathroom's at the end of the hall, if you want to fix your makeup or anything."

I suspected that was a hint and took him up on the suggestion.

When I'd finished, the bedroom door was closed and there was no sign of Rev. His minute had obviously stretched into several, so I wandered along to the living room to renew acquaintances with Tweetie.

He wasn't in his cage.

I gazed about the room, thinking Rev must sometimes leave him out to fly around. The last thing I wanted to do was step on him.

Then Rev came striding in from the hall. There had to be an ensuite bath because his wet hair said he was fresh from the shower. That started me feeling grubby again.

He'd changed into jeans and a creamy cotton sweater that made his shoulders look extremely broad.

"What's up?" he said.

"I was just looking for Tweetie."

Rev glanced at the cage, then frowned, muttering, "How did he get out with the door closed?"

"You mean you didn't leave him out this morning?"

"I never leave him out. I never even *let* him out. He's a birdbrain. He'd probably fly straight into a window and bash himself to death."

I focused on the cage again, an uneasy thought wriggling its way through my mind . . . a *ridiculous,* uneasy thought. I was never going to read another word from those Egyptian books of Rev's.

"I guess he's not small enough to make it out even between the bars, is he?" I tried.

"No. So how the hell did he get out?" Rev glanced at me as if he thought I might actually have an answer. "What?" he said. "What are you thinking?"

"Nothing."

"Yes, you are. I can tell."

"Nothing, really. I mean, just something absurd."

"What? You're thinking that little bird-*ba* of Princess Amonit's flew all the way up to San Francisco and sprung Tweetie?"

"Not quite *that* absurd. It was just something else I read in one of your books last night."

"You know, I'm getting damned sorry I lent them to you," he said, giving me a wry smile to show he was teasing. "What's got you going this time?"

I shrugged, but I suspected there was no way Mr. Persistence would let this drop until I came clean.

"What?" he said again, confirming my suspicion.

"Well . . . it doesn't really have anything to do with Tweetie. I only thought about it because he's a canary. But that archaeologist who discovered King Tut's tomb?"

"Howard Carter?" Rev said.

"Right. When he was working in the tomb, cataloging its treasures, he kept a canary with him. On the same principle miners used. If the oxygen level got low, the canary would die because of its small lungs. Then Carter would know he had to get out."

"And did his canary die?"

"Well . . . yes, but not from lack of oxygen. One day, Carter came into the tomb and the cage was empty. With its door still closed."

Rev glanced at the closed door of Tweetie's cage, then back at me. "And?"

I shrugged again, aware I was sounding sillier with every word.

"And the cage was empty. . . ." Rev prompted.

"And it turned out there was a snake inside the tomb," I told him. "A cobra. It must have stuck its head through the bars of the cage and eaten the canary."

Slowly, Rev grinned.

"I'm only repeating a story," I protested. "A very well-known one, I gathered."

"Yeah, I vaguely remember something about it," he said, dropping to his haunches and making a big production out of surveying the living room floor.

I didn't think that was the slightest bit humorous. I wouldn't have mentioned the dumb story at all if he hadn't pressed. "I wasn't actually thinking there might be a snake in here," I muttered. "It was just the coincidence of the empty cage."

"Yeah," Rev said. He stood up, still wearing his annoying grin. "A snake getting into a tomb in Egypt is one thing. Getting into a third-story apartment in San Francisco would be something else."

"Well, actually, they figured somebody *put* the cobra inside the tomb. To kill Howard Carter."

Rev's grin faded and he rubbed his jaw, his gaze sweeping the floor again.

This time, I noted with a twinge of satisfaction, he looked anxious.

"Why don't you sit down for a minute," he said at last. "I'd better have a quick look around for Tweetie before we leave. Maybe he's gotten himself stuck someplace."

"I'll help."

"All right. You work your way along this side of the room, and I'll take the other side."

I didn't need much in the way of detecting skills to tell Rev was worried. And I didn't think it was simply because Tweetie might have gotten himself stuck someplace. It was because Rev couldn't figure how the bird had gotten out of the cage on its own.

He looked over at me and firmly said, "We're *only* looking for Tweetie, you know."

"Of course." And I sure as hell hoped he was all we found.

WE DIDN'T TURN UP a snake, but we didn't turn up any trace of Tweetie, either. Not so much as a single little yellow feather.

Even with my vivid imagination, I couldn't concoct an explanation for the bird's disappearance. Not one that didn't involve a snake, at least. Either that or someone having been in Rev's apartment while we were in L.A., but he claimed absolutely no one except him had a key.

Strangely, my first thought when he told me that was that it meant he had no significant woman in his life.

"The damned bird's *got* to be here someplace," Rev muttered.

"We *could* try the den," I said. It was the only room we hadn't searched.

"There's no way he can be in there," Rev said. "The door's been closed all day."

"But he isn't anywhere else. Maybe there's a little hole in one of the walls or something."

Rev gave me a withering look that said his apartment didn't have any walls with holes in them, but he opened the door to the den.

Inside, the message light on his answering machine was flashing.

He pushed the Play button and a woman's voice said, "Rev? Scott tried to get you at the office. Said it was important. You might want to give him a call tonight."

"That's Rachel, my secretary," Rev said. "Scott is her boyfriend."

The next voice up was a man's. "It's Scott Usher, Rev. Rachel told me you were in L.A., but you want to give me a call when you get in? Doesn't matter how late. That Obregon guy from Sherwin McNee has been at the Donner all day again today and…well, give me a call."

The machine went through a beeping routine, indicating there were no more messages. Rev shot me an uneasy glance as he pressed the Rewind switch.

"Rachel's boyfriend is also your friend at the Donner," I guessed. "The one who called you yesterday."

"Yeah. Last year, I was looking for a secretary while Rachel was looking for a job. Scott suggested I interview her."

"I wonder what he wants to tell you about Charlie this time?"

Rev simply shrugged, saying, "I'll phone him later." He glanced around the den, then shook his head. "Tweetie isn't in here. There's no point looking."

"Well, he must have just gotten in somewhere we missed," I said.

Rev nodded, but he obviously wasn't any more convinced of that than I was.

"Look," I went on, "I've kind of lost my appetite. So let's pass on dinner. I'll just call a taxi and you can keep hunting for Tweetie."

"No, I'll drive you. It won't take long."

We headed back down to Rev's car. The trip to my place should have taken ten minutes. With Rev at the wheel, it took six.

Even so, I caught him checking the rearview about fifty times. And I doubted he was hoping to catch sight of Tweetie flying along after the Porsche. He was probably experiencing the same kind of free-floating anxiety that I was.

It had been a strange, strange day. I only hoped it wasn't a prelude to a strange night.

Rev pulled into the No Standing zone in front of my apartment building and cut the engine, saying, "I'll see you up."

I'd normally have told him not to bother. It was only dusk and my street is pretty safe. But tonight I felt glad of an escort.

Mrs. Richey, the little old lady who lives in the main-floor front apartment, was hovering near the mailboxes when I paused to check mine.

She's lonely and loves to chat. And she manages to be near the front door so often when tenants arrive home that I'm sure she spends a lot of time watching for us through her living-room window.

Tonight, though, she had a valid reason for her hovering.

"This came for you today, dear. By messenger," she added, handing me an envelope from Sherwin McNee.

I thanked her and shoved it into my bag with a quick, guilty glance at Rev. I knew what it was. After I'd gotten home, yesterday, I'd called Research and asked them to check on the financial health of Careful Wheels.

The more I'd seen, the more I'd suspected Charlie was wrong about the company having cash-flow problem. And if he was, there was no obvious motivation for Rev to have stolen the mummy case.

I introduced Mrs. Richey to Rev, who'd clearly piqued her curiosity, and she managed to get in seven or eight questions before I edged him along to the stairs.

"Wow," he whispered as we started up them, "she'd have been great during the Spanish Inquisition. Do you get that sort of reception all the time?"

"Not *all* the time," I said, laughing quietly. "But she does have a good track record."

"She'd drive me nuts. I hate people asking me personal questions."

"You didn't really have to answer them. I usually manage not to. She hardly knows anything about my life. But aside from being a little nosy, she's really sweet."

"That's what you call a little nosy?" Rev muttered.

"*And*," I continued, ignoring his question, "she can be a godsend when there's a delivery or a repair man coming. She's always at home, and I think everyone in the building has given her a key to their apartment."

We passed the second floor and continued on up. Coincidentally, my apartment is on the third floor, like Rev's. That, though, is where the coincidence ends.

Not that my place is what anyone would refer to as a "walk-up," either. But the building is from the twenties, so it has old charm rather than modern elegance.

And the apartments themselves are nothing like Rev's. His is all clean design and open spaces. Mine is loaded with nooks and crannies that, on the odd sleepless night, I'm sure have hobgoblins of various sorts lurking in them, waiting to pounce if I close my eyes.

Then, of course, there's the fact that Rev owns his apartment while I rent, which fits right in with his driving a shiny new Porsche and me, an old, no longer very shiny Mustang. Insurance companies aren't known for paying big salaries.

"Do you want me to come in for a minute?" Rev asked as I unlocked my apartment door. "Just to be sure you don't have an empty birdcage in your living room or anything?"

That made me smile, but I shook my head.

"Well..." He paused, shoving his hands into the pockets of his jeans. "I've got to go into the office in the morning, touch base with Rachel and catch up on whatever I missed today. But I still want to hang in with you, Marina, and help get to the bottom of this."

"I'm not sure what Charlie's going to want me to do tomorrow." I also wasn't sure whether I wanted Revington York hanging in with me any longer or not.

I had a hundred and forty-three mixed feelings about this situation. I wanted to discuss some of them with Charlie Obregon, and make sure he still figured the idea of having our prime suspect tagging along made sense.

"Well, look," Rev said. "How about giving me a call at Careful Wheels in the morning? After you've talked to Charlie. Let me know where we go from here. I'll be able to free up whatever time I need."

I nodded.

Rev stood rocking back and forth on his heels for a moment, looking at me.

And then he rocked a little further forward and stopped. He leaned down and gently brushed his lips against mine.

I was so taken aback I didn't move. I simply stood there like a dummy while he kissed me.

It was, I realized hazily, a very nice kiss. His lips were gentle yet exciting at the same time, sending an electric tingle all the way to my toes.

It probably would have been been an utterly stupendous kiss if I'd actively participated.

He finally drew away, his blue eyes sparkling with warmth, and brushed his knuckles gently down my cheek. They felt strong and sure against my skin.

The combination of his touch and the most devastating smile I'd ever seen sent another tiny electric jolt through me.

"So," he murmured, "you'll call me after you've talked to Charlie?"

"Right," I managed to answer. I pushed the door open and stepped backward, into my apartment. "I'll call you after I've talked to Charlie."

I closed the door and stood leaning against it, my heart pounding like crazy. Suddenly, I had a hundred and forty-*four* mixed feelings about this situation. Number one hundred and forty-four, though, definitely wasn't one I wanted to discuss with Charlie Obregon.

Thinking about Charlie started me thinking about the phony mummy case again. The case with its modern mummy.

Wandering into the living room, I assured myself there was absolutely no chance I'd just been kissed by a murderer. Even if that mummy did turn out to have been . . . well, I *hadn't* just been kissed by a murderer, regardless. My intuition said so, loud and clear.

The message light on my own answering machine was flashing. I eyed it for a moment, wondering again what that Scott fellow from the Donner wanted to tell Rev about Charlie today, then I switched the machine to play.

"Just checking in, dear," my mother's voice said. "Call us when you have a minute."

The message made me smile. I doubt she's consciously aware that she still thinks of me as twelve, rather than twenty-eight, but the way she checks up on me every couple of days, if I don't call home, doesn't leave much doubt.

I dialed the house, and she answered on the third ring.

When I told her about Charlie's giving me the chance to help investigate an important claim, she was half thrilled and half worried. Neither she nor my father are convinced the fraud squad is a safe place for their only child to be working.

Her concern made me glad I hadn't told her what *specific* claim I was working on. There was no knowing what the papers would be printing in their follow-up stories about the mummy case.

"But you didn't have any trouble in L.A., did you dear?" she was asking. "I'm glad I didn't know you were going there beforehand. There've been so many problems in that city."

"No, no trouble. Everything was just fine." I considered telling her about Revington York, but couldn't decide exactly what I'd say. So I simply listened while she caught me up on the past couple of days in her life.

After I hung up, I headed for the kitchen and stood staring into the fridge at my leftover chicken.

For a few horrible seconds, I imagined it covered in little yellow feathers. That made the idea of eating dead bird distinctly unappetizing.

I settled for a grilled cheese sandwich, reluctantly passing on the idea of having a dill pickle with it. The spiciness always kept me awake. If I was careful tonight, I might be able to avoid reruns of last night's nightmares.

There was an interesting program on television, but I couldn't keep my attention on it for more than half a minute at a time. My mind kept straying back to Revington York.

I really couldn't believe the man was guilty of anything more serious than parking violations. Or maybe I just didn't *want* to believe he could be.

But Charlie had been back at the Donner today, asking more of his questions. What if he'd learned something incriminating about Rev? What if that was what Rev's friend wanted to talk to him about?

More likely, I told myself, Charlie had gotten answers that had removed Rev from our list of suspects. Or that had at least knocked him out of the number one spot. But I sure would like to know exactly where things stood.

I glanced at the phone, trying to decide if Charlie would mind my calling him at home. He lived alone, so there was no wife to wonder about a strange woman phoning him at night.

According to Nat Fishbein, Charlie had been married once but it hadn't worked. Knowing Charlie, it was difficult to imagine anyone living with him for long.

Even though he had his faults, he was dedicated to his job. He might be glad if I phoned now. Maybe he was as anxious to hear about my trip to L.A. as I was to hear about *his* day.

I delayed the decision briefly, phoning a florist that stayed open late and ordering flowers for Nat Fishbein.

The clerk suggested putting some nasty-tempered snap-dragons in with the vicious tiger lilies. I knew Nat would get a kick out of that.

By the time I'd given my credit card number, I'd convinced myself it would make perfect sense to call Charlie tonight. Checking my book for his home number, I reached for the phone once more.

"So YOU DON'T THINK anyone in L.A. was involved at all?" Charlie said when I'd finished telling him about the trip.

"That was the impression we got. The more we talked to people there, the more likely it seemed the switch was made after the case reached the Donner."

"Or while the Careful Wheels guys had it."

I exhaled slowly. So much for Charlie's having crossed Rev's name off his list of suspects.

"Dammit," Charlie muttered. "Your trip was a waste of time and money then."

The *money* bit made me wince. Charlie knew about the airfare, but that outrageous charge for the airport limo was going to come as an unpleasant surprise.

"A real waste," he was going on, "because I could have used you *here* today, Marina. I still didn't get to everyone I have to talk to at the Donner."

"But did you find out anything useful? From the people you *did* talk to?"

"Oh, sure, I've got a whole briefcase here, packed full of notes. We can go over them tomorrow."

"No, I mean..." I paused, then made myself ask. "I mean did you learn anything that seemed to incriminate Revington York?"

"Uh-uh. But nothing that seemed to incriminate anybody else in particular, either. So, in my book, The Rev remains our prime suspect. But the main news of the day is that the autopsy results on the mummy are in. Marina . . . the woman *was* murdered."

My throat went dry, and goose bumps formed over my entire body.

"She was suffocated," Charlie went on. "Not long ago, although they couldn't fix an accurate date, what with the body's having been mummified and all."

"Who was she?" I whispered.

"They don't know yet. A woman in her twenties. But with the mummification, I gather they'll have to go the dental records route to do an ID."

An image of Revington York's face was floating before my eyes. I closed them but that only made it clearer.

"You going to be okay with this?" Charlie said. "You want me to pull you off the investigation? I'll understand if you do."

Quickly, I tried to decide whether I should take Charlie up on his offer. If I did, his opinion of me would probably sink even lower than it already was.

I rested my hand on my mummy beads, picturing the smile on Rev's face when he'd convinced me to take them.

Revington York might still be the prime suspect in Charlie's book, but he wasn't in mine. And I was getting the craziest feeling that it was critical I help figure out who was *really* guilty.

"Charlie, I'll be fine staying on the investigation," I told him, trying not to sound as nervous as I felt. "I hate to leave anything half finished."

"Well..." he said, "if you're sure. But for Pete's sake, watch your step. And now that we know we're talking murder, forget all about the idea of getting close to Revington York. I don't want you anywhere near him. Hell, I don't even want you talking to him on the phone."

"Ahh...Charlie, I promised I'd call him after I spoke to you. He wanted me to let him know what was on for tomorrow. He's expecting to keep tagging along with me."

"Well call him this once, then. Say you have to help me at the Donner tomorrow and that I don't want him there. Tell him I said it would look strange, having someone from outside Sherwin McNee with us. But if there are more dealings with him, and I'm sure there will be, I'll handle them."

"Fine. I'll stay away from him." And I certainly would, just in case.

At least, I would until this investigation was wrapped up. But my intuition was at it again, this time telling me that, in the long run, I wouldn't be staying away from him at all. Provided he wasn't a thief and murderer, of course.

"Okay," Charlie said. "So you meet me at the Donner in the morning."

"What time?"

"Say about ten-thirty. I have to go into the office for a couple of hours first. I've got some things to take care of there, but there's no point in your coming in and waiting around for me."

"Okay, ten-thirty at the Donner."

"Give you a chance to sleep in."

"Thanks, I'll enjoy that." Assuming, I silently added, that my sleep wasn't fraught with nightmares full of murdered mummies and flying *ba*s and vanishing canaries.

I sat staring at the phone after I'd hung up, trying to decide if I should phone Rev tonight or wait till the morning.

Not that I wanted to make the call either time. He'd demand to know why Charlie was booting him off the case, and I didn't think he'd buy Charlie's "looking strange" explanation.

But if I didn't call now, I'd probably spend half the night worrying about what I was going to say.

I considered my options for a few minutes, then checked the Research file for Rev's home number and dialed it.

Surprisingly, his machine picked up. I breathed a sigh of relief that I could simply leave a message. I did so and then hung up, absently wondering where Rev was. If I hadn't phoned, it would never have occurred to me that he wouldn't be at home, looking for Tweetie some more.

Chapter Six

When I woke the next morning, I recalled with a sleepy smile that I didn't have to race madly around getting ready for work.

Every now and then, Charlie does something uncharacteristically kind. And telling me not to bother going into the office before meeting him definitely qualified.

I propped myself up on one elbow and lay gazing out into the fog. As always, in the summer months, it had rolled in from the Pacific overnight, filling the Bay and shrouding the city in its damp, gray chill.

Even in July, San Francisco's average daily high is only in the mid-sixties, and the mornings are far cooler. The benefit is that the cold makes for good sleeping, and I'd certainly slept well last night.

I hadn't had a single nightmare. Deciding not to eat that dill pickle with my sandwich had been a wise move.

In fact, I was going to swear off dill pickles for life, because what I'd had instead of nightmares was a long, delicious dream in which Revington York had been kissing me. And in the dream, I hadn't stood there like a dummy. I'd kissed him back.

I climbed out of bed, thinking that the sooner somebody figured out who had *really* been behind switching those mummy cases, the better.

Not even one percent of my brain, and none of my intuition, believed Rev could be guilty. Before going to bed, I'd looked at the brief Research report Mrs. Richey had taken in for me yesterday.

Just as I'd suspected, the information about Careful Wheels having financial problems was faulty. After further digging, Research had decided the "serious cash-flow difficulties" were both temporary and not serious at all. Which meant that there'd been no desperate need for money to have turned Rev into a crook.

The researcher who'd compiled the data had included a note to me, saying he'd appreciate it if I could manage not to mention the goof to Charlie. I'd have to think about that.

I'd also have to think about what I'd promised Charlie: that I wouldn't go anywhere near Revington York. But, as long as there was still that tiny, little possibility... well, I guess it wouldn't hurt to stay away from Rev. For the moment, at least.

I wandered into the kitchen, made coffee, then sat with it in the living room, absently trying to assess the decor with an impartial eye. Even though it didn't look like something out of a designer's magazine, the way Revington York's living room did, I liked it.

The furniture was traditional. A lot of it had come from my parents' house, during my mother's last redecorating frenzy. So the pieces weren't very new, but they were good quality and she'd chosen them with love.

The phone started to ring, interrupting my thoughts. I was strongly tempted to let my machine pick up. Odds were ten to two it was Rev, wanting a fuller explanation of the message I'd left for him last night.

As much as I'd have liked to hear his voice, I didn't relish the prospect of trying to explain, in detail, why Charlie didn't want him working with me. He'd been upset enough at learning Charlie suspected him of being the mummy case thief, let alone being suspected of murder.

After two rings, my desire to hear Rev's voice won out and I reached for the phone.

"Marina?" a man said when I answered.

"Yes?"

"Marina, this is Homer Leibranch."

For a second I didn't put the name together with the man, because his calling me at all, let alone at home, was so improbable. Mr. Leibranch is a senior vice president at Sherwin McNee, and Charlie Obregon's boss.

"Marina?" he said again.

"Yes... sorry... you took me by surprise."

"Yes, well, I'm afraid I have something unfortunate to tell you. We're trying to reach everyone in Special Claims before they hear about it on the news. Marina, Charlie Obregon is dead. It happened early this morning. He started his car and a bomb exploded. Somebody planted it during the night and..."

Mr. Leibranch kept talking but I stopped listening. My eyes were stinging with tears. I'd begun to hyperventilate.

I cradled the receiver against my shoulder and cupped my hands over my mouth, trying to breathe.

"Are you there, Marina? Are you all right?"

"Yes," I whispered, even though I was anything but all right. I was in total, utter panic.

Nat Fishbein had a rule about never jumping to conclusions. But it wasn't much of a jump to think that somebody had murdered Charlie because of the questions he'd been asking about the mummy case.

Mr. Leibranch was speaking again, so I tried to tune into what he was saying.

"I'll be getting on top of everything that's happening in Special Claims as quickly as I can," he said. "In the meantime, I'm telling people to simply proceed with what they're working on. And you've been helping Charlie with the mummy case investigation, right?"

I'd gotten my breathing almost back to normal and managed to say, "Yes. I...I was supposed to meet him at the Donner later this morning. Help him finish questioning people there."

"Well, look, I made a quick check of his office, and there's nothing in it on that claim."

"I think he had everything at home. I spoke to him last night, and he said he had a whole briefcase full of notes."

There was a funny little throaty noise, then Mr. Leibranch said, "Well, I'm afraid his briefcase went with him. So I guess we'll have to go back to square one."

I mumbled something that didn't make sense even to me. My mental picture of Charlie's car exploding was growing more and more vivid, and I couldn't think past it.

"Marina," Mr. Leibranch finally said, "I realize this is a shock. And I know you're not really ready to work on your own. I'll get someone experienced on this with you as soon as I can. In the meantime, you're the only one who knows anything about the claim, so just do your best. Hold on a minute."

I held on, my head spinning and a sick feeling in my stomach.

Leibranch finally came back on the line, saying, "Sorry about that, but the police are here and I knew they'd want to talk to you. They're assuming Charlie's death might be related to what he's been working on, so they've already sent detectives to the Donner. The fellow here says that since that's where you were going, anyway, that's where they'll interview you. When you get there, you're to ask for a Detective Frank Barboni. He'll be expecting you."

"Detective Frank Barboni," I repeated numbly.

"Ahh...Marina, listen. The more I think about this...maybe, the way things stand, you shouldn't try to do anything at the Donner today. See what you think once you're there. But maybe, after you've seen Barboni, you should just come into the office. Or go on home if you're in rough shape. The claim can wait for a day or two."

I sat staring into space after I'd hung up, trying to slow the thoughts that were whirling crazily around in my head.

Charlie Obregon had been murdered. By someone who didn't like the questions he'd been asking at the Donner.

I closed my eyes against the thought, but it wouldn't go away.

Maybe I *had* been kissed by a murderer.

After all, Rev hadn't liked the questions Charlie had been asking one little bit. I could hear Rev's voice as clearly as if he were sitting beside me.

"What the hell are people going to think?" he'd snapped the other day. "With your damned boss running around implying I planned the whole thing.

Somebody has to shut the guy up before he ruins my reputation."

Well, somebody *had* shut Charlie up.

I swallowed over the lump in my throat and tried to recall, word for word, the message Rev's friend from the Donner had left on his machine.

Scott something was the guy's name. And he'd wanted to tell Rev what Charlie had been up to yesterday.

Rev would have returned Scott's call last night, after he'd driven me home. And later, when I'd phoned Rev, he hadn't been in his apartment.

I closed my eyes again, my entire body trembling. Someone had planted a bomb in Charlie's car last night.

And it could have been Revington York.

I MADE IT AS FAR as the parking lot behind my apartment building, then simply sat in my trusty old Mustang for a long, long time. I'd put the key in the ignition but was afraid to turn it.

"You're being ridiculous," I muttered to myself at last. But I got out of the car, opened the hood and stood staring, anyway.

As far as I could tell, everything looked the same as usual. But, despite my years in Auto Claims, most of what I know about cars involves makes, models and values.

I'm definitely no mechanic. The most I ever do is check my oil. And I had no idea whether car bombs were easy to see or got hidden away under an engine part.

"Problems?"

The voice made me jump, but it belonged to Craig Renfrew, one of my neighbors. Craig has a Trans Am and seems to spend half his life lying under it, fiddling with all those things people fiddle with under cars.

"Ahh...it was coughing a little the other day," I said. "Does everything look all right to you?"

He gave a cursory once-over, saying, "You can't tell much from just looking. But I don't see any loose wires or anything. If you're lucky, it's only a little dirt in the gas line. That'll clear itself."

I managed a smile of thanks and got back into the driver's seat.

Once Craig was out of what I figured would be flying debris range, I screwed up my courage and turned the key.

The engine purred to life and my heart began to slow to normal speed.

The Donner Museum is out near San Francisco State, a fair distance from North Beach, and by the time I got there I'd stopped shaking. But just barely.

I turned in at the sign for museum parking, took a ticket from the machine and started down the ramp.

And then I began shaking all over again.

Partway to the museum, I'd noticed a car that seemed to be following me. A green Honda Accord with darkly tinted glass. At first I'd written it off as a combination of nerves and imagination, but there it was in my rear-view again. It had turned into the parking garage after me and was directly on my tail.

My bag was sitting on the seat beside me. Frightened half to death, I fumbled in it, worked my snub-nosed .38 out of its zippered compartment, and put the gun on my lap.

I had to drive down three levels before I spotted an empty space. By that time, I was sure there was a machine gun pointed at me from behind the Honda's dark glass.

I pulled into the space, then picked up my .38 and turned around in the seat, hoping to catch the license number if I didn't get blown away.

The Honda drove on by, without a single round of machine gun fire, and disappeared down to the next level. The angles hadn't worked right for me to get even a glimpse of the number.

Before unlocking my car door, I looked around carefully. Underground lots make me nervous at the best of times, and this certainly wasn't the best of times.

Telling myself there were probably twenty cops upstairs in the museum, I put my gun back where it belonged and hurried along between the two rows of parked cars to the elevator.

Almost the first person I saw when I stepped off it, into the entrance foyer of the Donner, was Revington York. My feet froze to the floor and my heart started pounding double time.

He was wearing jeans and a navy turtleneck, and the words *dark* and *dangerous* popped into my head again. Just as they'd done the very first time I'd seen him.

He spotted me at the same instant I saw him and began striding purposefully across the marble floor toward me.

From somewhere deep inside, a basic animal instinct urged me to get back on that elevator. But then I heard its doors swooshing shut behind me.

I stood my ground, reminding myself about those twenty cops. I could even see a couple of them, keeping an eye on the entrance.

Rev stopped in front of me, his gaze not wavering from mine, his hands half raised at his sides, as if he wanted to take me by the arms but was holding himself back. "You're all right," he said.

I simply nodded.

"I wanted to be sure. When I got to my office, Rachel told me about Charlie. The word spread like wildfire around here, and Scott had called to tell her. I tried phoning you but got your machine, so..."

Rev paused, running his fingers through his hair. "The message you left me last night said you'd be coming here this morning. And as I said...well, I wanted to be sure you were all right."

"Just kind of shaky," I managed to say, wondering if Rev was really here out of concern for me, or if he'd come because he wanted something else. And if so, what?

He gazed into my eyes for another minute, then swore so quietly I scarcely heard him. "You think I had something to do with that bomb, don't you?"

I shook my head.

"Dammit, I was afraid you'd think that!"

"I don't know what I think," I said, trying to keep my voice even. I was upset and frightened. And I really *didn't* know what I thought.

"Dammit, Marina, I know I was mad about Charlie and his fool questions, but I sure as hell didn't go from being mad to killing the guy."

"Of course not," I murmured. "I...Rev, I'm supposed to check in with a police detective here. He's expecting me. I can't talk right now."

I tried to edge around Rev but he caught my arm. "Marina, listen to me. I didn't have anything to do with switching those mummy cases and I swear I didn't have anything to do with what happened to Charlie."

But the police would suspect he had.

Suddenly, it struck me. *That* might be why he'd really come here. What the *something else* he wanted could be. Maybe he thought he could convince me not to tell the cops about his outburst the other day, not tell them how angry he'd been at Charlie.

My mouth felt dry, and there were a hundred butterflies in my stomach. I didn't know whether Rev was putting on an act or not. And I didn't know if he'd had anything to do with Charlie's murder . . . but I couldn't rule it out.

I glanced anxiously around, wishing I'd never left my apartment. I didn't want to be at the Donner, and I didn't want to be with Revington York.

"I have to go," I said, pushing his hand from my arm.

"Marina, I've got to make you believe I didn't—"

"Just leave me alone," I said, stepping back from him. The total, utter panic I'd felt earlier this morning was threatening to swamp me again.

I had to get out of here. I was in no shape to talk to anyone, let alone a police detective. I'd go home, then call Detective Frank Barboni and set up something for later. But right now, I had to get out of here.

As if in answer to an unvoiced prayer, I heard the elevator doors opening behind me.

Quickly, I began moving backward, my eyes on Rev. If he followed, I wouldn't get on the elevator.

He didn't. He simply stood watching me, his mouth a thin, tight line.

I stepped into the elevator, still looking straight at him, and pressed P3.

By the time the elevator had descended three levels, I'd taken a lot of deep breaths. But when the doors opened again, I wasn't in much better shape than I'd been when they'd closed.

I'd never before been so rattled. Of course, I'd never before had a boss blown to smithereens.

Every time I thought about poor Charlie, tears began forming. I blinked hard, trying to clear my vision enough to check the area for suspicious-looking characters.

There were no characters in sight, suspicious-looking or otherwise, so I fumbled through my bag for my keys. For a moment I considered taking my gun out again, then told myself I was being absurd and started quickly in the direction of my car.

Often, when I'm afraid, I start feeling hot. And right now my temperature had to be a hundred and twelve. I lifted my hair off the back of my neck as I walked.

A strand caught around my mummy beads, pulling a little, and I realized I'd put them on again this morning without even thinking. Wearing them was already a habit.

When I reached the safety of my car, I opened the sunroof and cranked down the driver's window. Once I got outside, the constant wind that blows in the city would cool me off.

I was just leaning forward to put my key in the ignition when a hand grabbed my shoulder. My heart stopped.

"Don't move," Revington said into my ear. "Don't move a muscle."

Terrified, I gave my bag a sidelong glance. If I could just get to my gun . . .

But Rev had already taken his hand off my shoulder and was walking to the front of the car. He lifted the hood and leaned in beneath it.

When he straightened up again his face was white. "Get out of the car," he said. "Get out of the damned car. There's something under here that doesn't belong."

My hands were shaking so badly I could hardly get the door open.

By the time I had, Rev was beside it. He half dragged me out of the car, then stood with his arms wrapped tightly around me. If not for that, I suspected I'd have melted into a pool of relief on the concrete floor.

"What made you come after me?" I whispered when I thought I could manage to speak. "What made you think there might be something there?"

"I don't know," he murmured. "I just had a gut feeling."

I pressed my cheek against the reassuring strength of his chest, refusing to wonder if that could be a lie.

"WE'RE ALMOST DONE," Detective Barboni said, giving me a reassuring smile. "Just a thing or two more I want to cover."

His partner, Detective Rashkin, flipped back a few pages in her notebook and the two of them began talking quietly between themselves.

Rashkin was small, blond and pretty. Her face reminded me of a china doll's. She wore her fine hair pulled straight back, maybe in an attempt to look older, but it didn't help much. She must have whizzed through her time as a uniformed cop, because she was a Doogie Howser of detectives.

Since the moment Rev and I had met her, I'd been wondering if she felt as much like a rookie at her job as I did at mine. And if her working relationship with

Barboni was anything like mine had been with Nat Fishbein.

Not that Barboni was anything like Nat. Frank Barboni looked as Italian as his name sounded. And Barboni couldn't be more than in his early forties, while Nat was sixty. But Frank Barboni was clearly the teacher and Lisa Rashkin the pupil, like I'd been with Nat.

They were sitting on the opposite side of the museum's conference table from Rev and me. The table was so wide I could barely catch a word of what they were saying.

Rev leaned closer and rested his hand on mine for a moment, then sat back in his chair once more.

I tried to smile at him, but the best I could manage was a grade *F* smile. The something Rev had seen under my hood had turned out to be what Barboni called a gelignite explosive, wired to my ignition.

Exactly the same type of plastic device that had blown up Charlie's car.

Obviously, whoever had killed Charlie had tried to kill me. And the only obvious thing Charlie and I had in common was that we'd both been working on the mummy case claim.

I only wished the chain of the obvious extended to who had planted the bombs.

At least I knew it hadn't been Rev. He'd been in the museum with me while someone was down in the parking garage working on my car.

But I wasn't trying to fool myself that his being with me automatically put him in the clear. I hadn't spent six weeks in Nat Fishbein's company without learning not to dismiss even the smallest suspicion. And there was one that hadn't stopped niggling at my brain.

What if that bomb in my car had been a setup? So that Rev could rescue me and make me trust him implicitly.

Focus on opportunity and motive, Nat would say.

Well, Rev had known ever since he'd gotten my message on his machine last night that I was coming to the Donner this morning. Which took care of opportunity.

And as far as motive went, as long as I trusted him implicitly, he could continue staying close to me. Know what I was finding out.

That theory struck me as pretty farfetched, though. Especially after Rev's answers to some of Barboni's questions had filled in the blanks I'd wondered about.

Last night, when I'd phoned and Rev had been out, he hadn't been over at Charlie's planting a bomb. He'd been at his neighborhood Mexican restaurant, having the dinner I'd lost my appetite for.

There'd be witnesses to his having been there. The people who ran the restaurant knew him.

Of course, that didn't account for later on, but people who live alone seldom have witnesses to confirm that they were in bed all night.

And the message I'd overheard on Rev's machine hadn't been the big deal I'd thought it might be. Apparently, Scott Usher had simply wanted to let Rev know Charlie had been asking about him again. Nothing more than that. Unless Scott and Rev were somehow in this together.

I looked across at Barboni and Rashkin, still huddled over their notes.

Maybe the most important fact I'd learned from them was that the police were convinced the mummy cases had been switched *after* the authentic one had been delivered to the Donner.

They figured that Professor Reinhardt wasn't the type to turn crook after a lifetime spent walking the straight and narrow. And that, without his cooperation, the switch couldn't have been made at the L.A. end.

And as far as Careful Wheels was concerned, the cops had apparently never seriously considered Rev or his men suspects.

When I thought about it now, I could see that the idea of them stopping a moving van in broad daylight and shifting crates in and out of it *was* a little farfetched. Of course, the police hadn't seen Research's faulty report to make them think Rev might have had a financial motive.

Still, just because he wasn't on their list didn't make me a hundred percent comfortable about trusting him implicitly. After all, cops weren't perfect. And we were talking murder here. What if I did start trusting Rev completely when I shouldn't? It could be a fatal mistake.

"All right," Barboni said, finally glancing up. "Let's go over the details about that car one more time. Try to picture it, Marina. Was there anything else at all? A scratch? A broken taillight? Anything?"

They figured the green Honda was the key. Whoever was in it had followed me to the museum, the theory went, then planted the bomb while I was upstairs.

It was a logical conclusion. The parking lot behind my apartment is too public for anyone to have risked tampering with my car. The museum's lot isn't. But recognizing the logic wasn't jogging my memory in the slightest.

"A green Honda Accord," Barboni prompted. "With darkly tinted glass. And you noticed it ... ?"

"Maybe halfway from my apartment to here. But the glass was practically black. So dark that I couldn't even see how many people were inside, let alone anything about them. You know, there *is* something I forgot to mention."

Rashkin poised her pen over her notebook, eyeing me expectantly.

"It crossed my mind that the glass might be too dark to be legal. But then I decided it was probably the fog, and maybe the angle I was at to the windshield, that were causing the problem. At any rate, until we got into the parking garage, the car hung back too far for me to see the license number. It was a California plate. That's all I could tell. And then ... well, I just couldn't get a look at it once we were in the garage."

"Okay. And the year? You're *positive* it was this year's model?"

"I told you," I said. "I spent the last four years working on auto claims. I could distinguish a '55 Studebaker from a '56."

Barboni grinned. "I wish all our witnesses were as good as you. And you're positive you don't know anyone with a new Accord?"

"No. Not a green one, at least. And not one with tinted glass like that."

"You should have blown out the damned glass," Rev muttered. "When it drove past you, you should have blown out the damned glass. Then we'd have known who was in the car."

"I wasn't *positive* it was following me," I pointed out, trying not to smile. Rev was sounding like a character from a B gangster movie.

He'd been darned surprised to learn I have a gun, but now that he knew, he sure wasn't wasting any time thinking up uses for it.

"All right," Barboni said, "this will really help. We'll start checking registrations of new green Accords. And records of auto glass tinting companies. Only problem is, the car may turn out to have been stolen."

He shoved himself out of his chair, saying, "So, I guess that's it for now. Here's my card, Marina. Division headquarters can get hold of me anytime. Call if you remember anything else. Or if anything at all suspicious happens."

"What?" Rev said. "You aren't assigning officers to protect her? For God's sake, somebody just tried to kill her."

Barboni gave him a dark look, saying, "I'll mention it to my CO. I'd already intended to. But he's bound to say no. He's got a manpower problem, and watching over someone three shifts a day, seven days a week, takes a lot of manpower."

"So she's just supposed to wander around on her own?" Rev demanded.

Barboni gave him an even darker look, then turned to me. "You're licensed to carry that gun of yours, so keep it with you at all times. And keep an eye on everything that goes on around you. I'll notify the North Beach area right away. They'll have their patrol cars make regular sweeps past your apartment building."

"Terrific," Rev snapped. "That's sure to prevent the guy from killing her."

"Would you like me to have an officer drive you someplace?" Barboni asked, ignoring Rev.

After they'd removed the bomb, the police had towed my Mustang away to check it for possible evidence, and it would be a couple of days before I'd have it back.

"I'll drive her," Rev was saying.

Barboni glanced me a question about that.

I hesitated for a second. I definitely wanted *someone* to give me a ride. I didn't want to be alone. So my choice was Rev or a cop I didn't know.

And Rev had saved my life only a couple of hours ago. If he wanted me dead, he'd merely have had to let that bomb do its thing. And he sure wasn't going to harm me when the cops knew he was with me. Besides, I did have my gun.

"I'll probably feel better if Rev drives me," I told Barboni. "But thanks for the offer."

Rev shot me a smile that made me glad I'd decided the way I had. Not that it meant I'd decided I was going to start trusting him completely. At least, not until that last niggling little suspicion was gone.

But if, against all odds, Rev did turn out to be one of the bad guys... well, Charlie had wanted me to help figure out who they were. And after what had happened to Charlie, it would mean a lot to me if I could deliver for him.

"Where will you be if we need to reach you later today?" Barboni asked.

I thought rapidly. Homer Leibranch had suggested I go home if I was in rough shape, and that defined the shape I was in. But maybe I'd be better off in the office.

"I think I'll go into work," I said at last. "At least for a while."

"Good idea," Rev offered. "That'll give you the chance to bring whoever's going to take over this claim up to speed. And it'll keep your mind occupied."

"I'm not sure anyone else will be taking over," I told him. "What Leibranch said was that he'd get someone experienced on it *with* me."

"He said that before somebody tried to kill you," Rev said. "You sure as hell can't keep working on it. You'd still be a murder target if you did."

I caught the glance that passed between Detectives Barboni and Rashkin but couldn't read it. "Is Rev right?" I asked.

Barboni cleared his throat, then said, "Well . . . in a way he is. And you probably *should* pull yourself off the claim. Otherwise, you'll be looking over your shoulder a hundred percent of the time."

I eyed Barboni closely, aware he hadn't actually answered my question, but he didn't volunteer anything more.

"What did you mean that Rev was right *in a way?*" I tried.

"Well . . . he's right that you'd definitely be a murder target if you kept on doing what you're doing."

"But?" I persisted when he hesitated.

He shrugged unhappily. "But the trouble is that somebody already thinks you know too much. And you aren't going to stop knowing it just because you stop working on the claim."

"You mean . . . whoever tried to kill me is going to try again . . . no matter what I do?"

"I mean they might, no matter what you do," Barboni said.

Chapter Seven

"That's sure a damned cavalier attitude toward people's lives," Rev was muttering as we headed along level two of the garage.

I glanced at the officer Detective Barboni had assigned to escort us to Rev's car, hoping he hadn't heard. He wasn't reacting, but that was no guarantee.

"They should be guarding you around the clock," Rev went on.

I didn't say anything. The idea certainly appealed to me, but I couldn't see it happening.

This wasn't the movies, it was real life. And I knew the manpower shortage problem Barboni had mentioned was real as well.

There was another officer standing next to Rev's Porsche when we came in sight of it. He nodded to the three of us, then started off.

"We took the liberty of checking your car over, Mr. York," the cop with us said.

"Without setting off the alarm?" Rev demanded. "The system's supposed to be fail-proof."

The cop shrugged. "We've got a couple of guys who can disarm them. Which means it's not impossible. So, as I said, we checked it over. Just in case."

The remark, meant to reassure us, only made me more anxious. I hadn't been thinking about someone planting a bomb in the Porsche, but now I was.

We thanked the officer and climbed into the car.

"Let's get out of this place," Rev said, clicking the locks down, then starting the engine. He backed out of the space and wheeled toward the exit.

"We're going to Sherwin McNee?" he asked as we waited for the parking attendant to make change from a twenty.

I nodded. "I think you were right. I'll be better off keeping my mind occupied."

Rev tossed his change into the glove compartment, and pulled out onto Ocean Avenue.

We drove several blocks in silence, aside from the throaty growl of the car itself, until Rev said, "So what are you going to do?"

"What Barboni suggested, I guess. Carry my gun and keep an eye on whatever's happening around me. There's not much else I *can* do."

I'd succeeded in sounding nonchalant enough to almost fool myself. But what I really wanted to do was crawl into bed and hide under the duvet until the police had Charlie's murderer in jail.

"There's a *whole lot* else you could do," Rev was saying. "For starters, you could hire a bodyguard."

"And pay *him* instead of my rent?" I said, shooting a dim look across the car.

"Well . . . you could move out of your apartment for a while, then. Whoever this guy is, he followed you this morning, so he knows where you live."

I'd realized that, of course, but I'd been trying not to think about it. It's bad enough when I imagine hobgoblins lurking in my apartment's nooks and crannies.

Tonight I was going to be imagining murderers. Or, worse yet, they might be real.

"So?" Rev said. "You could go stay with your parents for a while."

"Uh-uh. The moment I told them I was moving to Special Claims, they started worrying that I wouldn't be safe. If I told them what was going on, they'd lock me in a room and throw away the key. I'm serious," I added when Rev's glance said he thought I was exaggerating. "I'm an only child, and they haven't quite accepted the fact that I grew up."

"Well, then, go stay with a friend."

"Oh, sure. What do I say when I ask? 'Okay if I come stay with you for a few days, or weeks, or months, because there's a murderer after me? And I don't want to be alone if he shows up?' Nice friend I'd be."

Rev didn't reply for a minute, then he said, "All right, come and stay with me."

"What?" I looked over as I spoke, expecting to see he was joking.

He gazed back at me, not smiling. "Marina, I don't mean come play house with me, okay? It's just that I've been in this with you almost from square one. And now that it's turned into a mess for you I feel kind of...well, the point is that if this guy tries anything more you wouldn't be alone. That couch in my den is a pullout. And the security in my building is better than in yours."

I had to admit that was true. The front door of my building has a tendency not to click locked after people, and my neighbors are lazy about checking that it has. Which means the security consists mainly of old Mrs. Richey's watchful eyes.

"So...the idea makes sense, doesn't it?" Rev pressed.

For a crazy second I was almost tempted to take him up on the offer. But there were so many reasons not to that I didn't even bother enumerating them in my head.

"Thanks," I said, "but no."

Rev gave me a tight-lipped look of annoyance.

After a few more silent blocks, he said, "As soon as we get to Sherwin McNee, you're going to talk to this Leibranch guy, right? Tell him you want off the mummy case claim?"

I closed my eyes and leaned back against the headrest. "I don't know," I said at last. "I'll see what he thinks."

"Marina . . ."

I opened my eyes again. I'd never heard my name spoken in such a menacing tone. The only person who'd even come close was my father. And that had been ten years ago, after I'd crunched his brand new car by backing into a pole.

"I'll see what Mr. Leibranch thinks," I said firmly.

"Leibranch didn't almost get blown up," Rev snapped.

"No . . . but you heard what Barboni said. Whatever this guy thinks I know, he's not going to figure I'll forget it if I stop working on the claim."

"Barboni *also* said that he thought you should pull yourself off the case."

"Look, I know somebody might be trying to kill me. I'm going to be looking over my shoulder whether I drop the case or not. So maybe I'd be better off hanging in. Maybe I can learn enough to figure out who the *somebody* is."

"That just might be the dumbest thing I've ever heard! You're not a cop. Hell, you're not even a private detective. You're an insurance adjuster. A *novice* adjuster, when it comes to a claim like this. And hanging in on it has *got* to increase the risk of something happening to you."

"Maybe you're right," I snapped. "But the sooner the cops get whoever killed Charlie the sooner I can relax. So if I can help... besides, I feel I owe Charlie."

Rev looked ready to tell me I was insane, but I shut him up with one of my best wordless glares. He might like being in charge of things, but he damned well wasn't in charge of my life. I'd decide whether I was hanging in or backing off. Not him.

Absently, I began fingering my mummy beads. And then the spookiest thing in the world happened. A gentle, silvery voice whispered in my ear.

"Do not give up," it murmured. "I am Princess Amonit, daughter of Ramses V, Pharaoh of all Egypt. Do not give up and I will help you."

I couldn't have dropped my hand to my lap faster if the beads had been red hot.

"What?" Rev said.

I glanced nervously at him.

"What?" he said again. "Marina, your face just lost every trace of color."

"Ahh... you didn't hear something, did you? Sort of a voice?"

His face took on the same expression it had taken on in the L.A. museum. Back when I'd told him that I'd seen a bird with a human head in the exhibit case. It was his "time to call the men in the white coats" expression.

Before I could think of what to say next, the quiet voice spoke once more.

"Do not give up," it whispered again. "As long as you wear my beads, you are safe. I can help and protect you."

I continued to stare at Rev, wondering if what he was thinking could be right. Maybe I *was* crazy.

Having a vivid imagination is one thing. But hearing voices? That's something else again.

Fearfully, I rested my hand on the mummy beads once more. An immediate feeling of calm washed over me.

"You see," the silvery voice whispered. "There is not a thing to be frightened of."

Not a thing, I thought, my throat dry. Except someone had tried to murder me a few hours ago. And now I was hearing the voice of an ancient Egyptian princess, telling me I was wearing *her* beads.

But why had she suddenly spoken to me? Because she knew I *had* been seriously thinking about giving up? That seemed like the logical conclusion, if there could be anything *logical* about hearing a disembodied voice.

Nothing Nat Fishbein had taught me in our six weeks together had prepared me for this. In fact, nothing in my entire life had prepared me for this.

I took a deep breath, my mind racing, then said, "Rev? These beads? You told me a note came with them."

"Uh-huh. Thanking me for doing a good job transporting the exhibit pieces. Why?"

"I was just wondering . . . do you still have it?"

"The note?"

"Yes."

For a second I thought he was going to say he'd thrown it out. Then I wouldn't know if there'd ever really been one at all, if he'd really been sent the beads as a gift or had gotten them by some other means.

But what he said was, "Sure, it's at the office. We keep a file of the letters we get complimenting the company. Use them as testimonials with prospective clients."

"Would you mind letting me see it?"

Rev grinned. "You a prospective client?"

I glanced out of the car, ignoring his teasing. We were on Market Street. It would take us right downtown, but we were only at Castro.

"Now?" I persisted, looking back at him. "Instead of going straight to Sherwin McNee, could we go by your office and see that note first?"

He gave me a puzzled look, but flicked on his signal and turned right onto Dolores and into the Mission district.

WHEN REV SLOWED the Porsche as we neared Careful Wheels, my mind was still spinning.

Every time I touched the mummy beads, I was rewarded with a sense of calm. But it had to be entirely my imagination at work. It was making me feel calm, just as it had made me hear the silvery voice.

People simply don't get messages by psychic express from a princess who's been dead for more than three thousand years.

And even if hearing her spirit speaking was possible, the voice had said I was wearing *her* beads. But I knew that wasn't true.

Mine were fake. A *reproduction* of Princess Amon-it's beads. From the gift store at the Donner, courtesy of the museum's public relations people. Rev had told me that.

I glanced uneasily at him as he pulled into the company lot and parked. For a moment, I suspended my disbelief and accepted that I'd really heard the voice of Princess Amonit. And then, given what she'd said, I also accepted that my beads were the real thing. Not a reproduction but the genuine article...stolen from Princess Amonit's missing mummy.

That possibility made me shiver so hard my teeth almost began to chatter.

"Cold?" Rev said, opening his door.

I shook my head, got out of the car and started after him, still trying to sort things out as we crossed the parking lot and headed along the street toward his office.

Rev had given me these beads. And if they *were* the real thing, how had he gotten them?

By being the brains behind the mummy case switch? Was he guilty, after all?

My thoughts were in such a tangle I wasn't sure what made sense, but for him to be guilty...well, the facts just didn't seem to add up to that.

The real mummy beads had to be worth a fortune. So if that's what these were, Rev would never have given them away so casually. If that's what they were, he'd never have invited me up to his apartment in the first place. Not when he had them sitting out in plain sight.

After all, I was working on the insurance claim. So I just might have realized what the beads were when I saw them.

But if they weren't the genuine article, if I couldn't explain what was happening to me as a paranormal experience—incredible as *that* was to believe—then what on earth was going on inside my head?

Rev opened the Careful Wheels door and held it for me.

This time, the outer office wasn't empty, and the reception desk wasn't threatening to overflow with papers.

The girl sitting there was obviously efficient, because everything was neatly arranged.

She was twenty-four or twenty-five and extremely pretty, with those sun-bleached-tanned-skin Southern California good looks that sometimes make me envious.

I know it's gullible to be duped by advertising campaigns, but I've always bought the story that blondes really *do* have more fun.

The glance she gave me was disinterested, but when Rev walked in behind me she flashed a zillion-watt smile.

He tossed his keys onto the top of the filing cabinet, then introduced her as his secretary, Rachel Windsor.

"And this is Marina Haine," he added, nodding toward me. "From Sherwin McNee Indemnity."

Rachel glanced at me again, no more friendly this time, but a touch more interested. Then she noticed the mummy beads and grew a lot more interested.

I smiled smugly at her. For someone who'd told Rev she thought they looked like junk when he'd offered them to *her,* she seemed darned annoyed that he'd given them to me.

"Rachel, I need that letter from the Donner," Rev said, "the one that came with the beads."

She dragged her eyes away from them and got up from behind her desk. In addition to everything else, she had that long, leggy build men drool over.

On second thought, I decided, realizing she was no taller than my own five-foot-six inches, her legs weren't really any longer than mine. Her skirt was just drawing attention to them.

It was black leather and extremely short. And, I thought, extremely out of season in July. It got even shorter when she opened a drawer of the filing cabinet and bent over.

I gave myself a mental slap on the wrist. Southern Californian good looks may sometimes make me envious, but they don't normally make me catty.

Glancing at Rev, I wondered if my cattiness could possibly have anything to do with the huge smile Rachel had given him.

I decided it hadn't. That would smack of jealousy, and I'd certainly never get jealous over a man I didn't completely trust.

Or a man who'd kissed me precisely once. Once wasn't enough to put me into a possessive frame of mind about *any* man.

Besides, I knew Rachel had a boyfriend. That Scott friend of Rev's at the Donner.

"Here we are," she said, turning back to Rev with yet another brilliant smile.

"Let Marina have a look at it," he told her.

She handed it over, her smile abruptly vanishing.

I studied the letter carefully. It was typed on museum letterhead and wasn't signed with a name—simply, "from public relations."

Basically, it said what Rev had told me it said. It thanked him for transporting the exhibit without a hitch, then went on to explain about the necklace they'd enclosed as a gesture of appreciation. It was one of several reproductions of items relating to the Egyptian exhibit. Things they'd had made up to sell in the museum gift shop.

"So?" Rev said at last. "You going to let me in on what you figure is so important about that?"

I tried to think of a reasonable explanation. I certainly wasn't going to tell Rev about hearing that voice, let alone tell him it had said I was wearing Princess Amonit's real necklace. Especially not in front of Rachel.

"I...ahh, actually, I just wanted to see *who* had thought to send the beads. The person's name, I mean. But, of course, this isn't personally signed."

"Why would the name matter?" Rev said.

"Oh...you know, all those questions I'll have to ask around the Donner now that Charlie's..." I shrugged. My well of words had run dry.

Fortunately, Rev didn't press and Rachel clearly couldn't have cared less.

"So," Rev said. "That's it? You want to head for Sherwin McNee now?"

"Why don't I call a taxi?" I said.

Rev shook his head.

"No, I really should. I don't want to take up your entire day."

What I actually didn't want was Rev knowing about the bizarre thought that had occurred to me. I wanted to check it out on my own, not with him along. If he knew what I was wondering about, he'd only be more certain I was nuts.

"I have nothing better to do," Rev said.

"You have all kinds of things to do," Rachel told him. "There's a big stack of messages on your desk. Almost two days' worth now."

Rev glanced from me to her, then back to me. "Come here," he said, grabbing my hand and half dragging me into his office. He shut the door behind us and leaned against it as if he figured I might try to escape.

"You've hatched some crazy new idea about what happened to the mummy case, haven't you?" he demanded.

"Not exactly," I said uneasily. The man was a clairvoyant!

"What do you mean, not exactly?"

"I didn't actually mean, not exactly. What I should have said was, no, I don't have any crazy new idea about what happened to the mummy case."

"But you've got a new idea about something, don't you? And you'd rather take a damned taxi than let me know what it is."

I stared at my shoes. He'd hit the nail smack on the head, but I didn't want to admit it.

"You aren't going to ask your Mr. Leibranch to take you off the mummy case claim, are you?"

My shoes were growing more fascinating by the second.

"I know you aren't," Rev continued. "Not the way you were mumbling about all those questions you were going to have to ask around the Donner since Charlie's gone. And you want to go back there right now, don't you? That's why you suggested calling a taxi. Because you want to go back to the Donner instead of to Sherwin McNee, and you didn't want me to know what you were up to."

"Rev, you've got work to do," I tried, waving lamely at his desk, at the stack of messages Rachel had mentioned. "And investigating the claim is *my* job, not yours."

"So you really *aren't* going to pull yourself off the damned claim."

I swore silently. He'd only been fishing, not mind reading, and he'd hooked me.

"I guess I'm not," I admitted.

Rev ran his fingers through his hair, gazing at me as if I was an incorrigible child.

"Look," he finally said, "let's get something straight between us, okay? Once and for all?"

"What?"

"I don't like your decision. But if you're not backing off this, then I'm not, either."

"Rev, why? It isn't *your* job."

He eyed me for another minute, then stepped forward, pulled me into his arms and gave me a long, hard kiss.

I pride myself on not making the same mistake twice, so this time I kissed him back.

And it turned out that I'd guessed right after the first time. My active participation made this one an utterly stupendous kiss.

"So," Rev whispered at last, kissing his way down my throat, "does that explain the why?"

"Pretty much," I murmured. "But would you mind just elaborating on the explanation a little?"

"Not at all." He nibbled his way back up to my lips and began elaborating.

WHEN REV AND I STOPPED for lunch on our way back to the Donner, it took until dessert arrived before I got up the nerve to explain exactly what I wanted to check out in its gift shop, and why.

Sometime in his office, while he'd been kissing me, my last niggling doubt about his innocence had disappeared. He'd won me over. I finally trusted him completely.

But trusting him and telling him something that was going to make me sound crazy again were two different things.

He'd obviously doubted my sanity yesterday, when I'd insisted it wasn't a normal bird I'd seen in that case at the L.A. museum. So the prospect of talking about the silvery voice and what it had said made me extremely uneasy.

He didn't interrupt once while I was telling him. When I finished, he sat slowly rubbing his jaw, still not speaking.

I took a big bite of my chocolate cheesecake, imagining the worst, wondering if he'd decided that kissing a crazy lady only makes her crazier.

Finally, he said, "I thought you didn't believe in that kind of stuff. I mean, when you figured you'd seen a human-headed bird, we agreed it couldn't really have been Princess Amonit's *ba*. We agreed your mind had to be playing tricks."

"I know what we agreed. But I didn't really...the voice was so real. And when I touch the beads...Rev, what if they *are* genuine?"

"They can't be."

I took another bite of cheesecake. It was delicious, but it wasn't making me feel any better about this discussion.

"Why the hell would anybody send me the real ones?" he demanded. "They could have sold them on the black market and made a bundle."

"Well...whoever has the real mummy is going to make a bundle, anyway. Unless they get caught, of course. I mean, the mummy case is priceless. Then there's the mummy herself. Don't forget the necklace wasn't the only thing of value wrapped in the linen. There was other jewelry. And amulets."

"But—"

"Rev, if these beads are the genuine article, somebody was trying to set you up. *That's* why they'd send them to you instead of selling them."

He stared across the table at me, not saying a word, so I continued. "Whoever switched those mummy cases knew someone was going to catch on. Sooner or later. Maybe they didn't expect Professor Reinhardt to be at the exhibit opening, but they had to know that when the phony was shipped back to L.A. he'd have spotted it was a fake."

Rev nodded for me to continue.

"And if the police found that you had the authentic beads in your apartment...the ones that came from Princess Amonit's mummy..."

"Dammit, Marina, you're right. If I had the beads, it would look like I'd had a whole lot to do with the switch. But who the hell sent them?"

"It could have been anyone who had access to the Donner's letterhead. Which probably means anyone who works there."

Rev began rubbing his jaw again, no longer looking skeptical.

"So what I want to do at the museum," I went on, "is see for sure if these beads are real or not. The reproductions will have been machine-made, so they'll all be absolutely identical. And if there's any difference between the necklace I'm wearing and all the others..."

"Let's go," Rev said, throwing a twenty onto the table and shoving himself out of the booth.

I gave the remaining half of my cheesecake a reluctant glance, then followed him out to the car.

Chapter Eight

The moment we pulled into the Donner's parking garage I started feeling queasy, and I doubted it had anything to do with what I'd eaten at lunch.

Only this morning, I'd almost been blown to kingdom come in here, and making a return visit this soon was pushing the limits of my courage.

Rev reached over and squeezed my hand. I rested the other on my mummy beads. The combination of his company and their calming effect went a long way toward making me feel less anxious.

When we got off the elevator at the museum's foyer, the police were still in evidence. In fact, we only made it halfway to the gift shop before Detective Barboni appeared. He zoomed in on us, wearing a puzzled expression.

"I thought," he said, focusing on me, "you were going back to your office for the day."

"I was. There's just something I wanted to...to look at in the gift shop."

His expression grew even more puzzled. "Well, I'd rather you didn't do any poking around here today. We won't be finished with the staff for a few more hours, and everyone already seems sick of answering questions. So maybe you could come back and do your thing tomorrow? Ask what you have to ask then?"

"Sure," I said, but I had no intention of spending from now until tomorrow wondering about my mummy beads. "I won't go anywhere except into the gift shop," I promised.

Barboni looked as if he were about to say no even to that, but Rev jumped in before he could open his mouth, saying, "Women, huh? Have you ever known one who wasn't born to shop? Marina says there's this thing she just *has* to buy for her mother's birthday party tonight. But I'll get her in and out of there in two minutes flat."

"Well . . ." Barboni said. "I guess, if you know what it is you want."

"Absolutely," I said. "I know exactly what I want."

Rev gave me a self-satisfied smile as Barboni turned away.

"For your information, I despise shopping," I snapped.

Rev shrugged, his smile growing even more annoying. "Worked, didn't it?"

I couldn't argue with that, so I simply tromped along beside him into the gift shop.

The necklaces weren't on display in the special section of items relating to the Egyptian exhibit.

We passed by the two regular jewelry counters without spotting them there, either.

"Where the hell are they?" Rev muttered.

"You don't suppose they could have sold out, do you?" I asked, worried that they might have. "The exhibit's been open for a week now."

PLAY THIS
MATCH GAME 3

with Big Money Prizes—you could
WIN UP TO $1-MILLION!
get Free Books and Surprise Gift, too

	STICK 1st	STICK 2nd	STICK 3rd
MATCH 3 you are instantly eligible to **WIN $10,000**	MATCH HERE	MATCH HERE	MATCH HERE
MATCH 3 you are instantly eligible to **WIN $35,000**	MATCH HERE	MATCH HERE	MATCH HERE
MATCH 3 you are instantly eligible to **WIN $1-MILLION**	MATCH HERE	MATCH HERE	MATCH HERE
MATCH 3 and get **FOUR FREE BOOKS**	MATCH HERE	MATCH HERE	MATCH HERE
MATCH 3 and get **A GREAT SURPRISE GIFT**	MATCH HERE	MATCH HERE	MATCH HERE

HERE'S HOW TO PLAY
"MATCH 3"

1 Detach this, your "MATCH 3" Game, & the page of stamps enclosed. Look for matching symbols among the stamps & stick all you find on your "MATCH 3" Game.

2 Successfully complete rows 1 through 3 & you will instantly & automatically qualify for a chance to win a Big Money Prize—up to a MILLION-$$$ in Lifetime Income ($33,333.33 each year for 30 years). (SEE RULES, BACK OF BOOK, FOR FULL PARTICULARS.)

3 Successfully complete row 4 & we will send you 4 brand-new HARLEQUIN INTRIGUE® novels—for FREE! These Free Books have a cover price of $2.99 each, but they are yours to keep absolutely free. There's no catch. You're under no obligation to buy anything. We charge nothing—ZERO—for your first shipment. And you don't have to make any minimum number of purchases—not even one!

4 The fact is, thousands of Readers enjoy receiving books by mail from the Harlequin Reader Service®. They like the convenience of home delivery...they like getting the best in romance fiction...and they love our discount prices!

5 Successfully complete row 5 &, in addition to the Free Books, we will also send you a very nice Free Surprise Gift, as extra thanks for trying our Reader Service.

6 Play the "Lucky Stars" & "Dream Car TieBreaker" Games also enclosed & you could WIN AGAIN & AGAIN because these are Bonus Prizes, all for one winner, & on top of any Cash Prize you may win!

YES! I've completed my "MATCH 3" Game. Send me any Big Money Prize to which I am entitled just as soon as winners are determined. Also send me the Free Books & Free Surprise Gift under the no-obligation-to-buy-ever terms explained above and on the back of the stamps & reply. (No purchase necessary as explained below.) 181 CIH ALAH

(U-H-I-01/94)

Name

Street Address   Apt. #

City   State   Zip Code
©1991 HARLEQUIN ENTERPRISES LTD.

Follow Directions & Return this Bonus Game

Scratch GOLD from both Box & Star on the   No purchase required. This Lucky Stars

TieBreaker

This is the Dream Car everybody's talking about–the Cadillac Fleetwood, loaded with extras. SCRATCH BOTH KEYS to find out if you are a Finalist to Win!

DREAM CAR

DREAM CAR

SCRATCH BOTH GOLD KEYS. IF #'S REVEALED MATCH, YOU'RE DEFINITELY A FINALIST IN THE TIEBREAKER TO SEE WHO WINS A NEW CADILLAC FLEETWOOD DREAM CAR!

BY BOTH & RETURN IN REPLY

any prize you may win in playing your "MATCH 3" Game!

PLAY THESE BONUS GAMES.. YOU COULD STILL WIN !!! MORE !!!

*PLAY &
YOU COULD
WIN A BIG*

LUCKY STARS

★ ★ ★

Everybody's got a Lucky Star & this may be yours. SCRATCH GOLD FROM BOX & STAR. If both match, you're definitely in - you qualify for a chance to win the Super Bonus Prize revealed!

Extra
EXTRA

Super
DOUBLE BONUS PRIZE

Prizes on these Games are BONUS EXTRAS, all for 1 winner, AND on top of

Use These Stamps
to Complete Your
"MATCH 3" Game

Simply detach this page & see how many matches you can find for your "MATCH 3" Game. Then take the matching stamps and stick them on the Game. Three-of-a-kind matches in rows 1 through 3 qualify you for a chance to win a Big Money Prize—up to a Million-$$$ . . .

. . . THREE-OF-A-KIND-MATCHES IN ROWS 4 & 5 GETS YOU FREE BOOKS & A NICE SURPRISE GIFT AS WELL! PLAYING IS FREE - FUN - EASY & THE WAY YOU COULD WIN! *PLAY TODAY!*

PLAY "MATCH 3" – YOU COULD WIN UP TO A MILLION–$$$ IN LIFETIME INCOME (YES, $1,000,000!) –GET FREE BOOKS & AN EXCITING SURPRISE GIFT, TOO!

★ Did you complete the first 3 rows of your "Match 3" Game? Did you print your name & address on the Game? Are you also playing & enclosing your Bonus Games? Please do, because so doing definitely qualifies you for a chance to win one of the Fabulous Prizes being offered, up to & including a MILLION–$$$ in Lifetime Income!

★ Did you complete rows 4 & 5? If you did, you are entitled to Free Books & a really nice Surprise Gift, as your introduction to our Reader Service. The Service does not require you to buy, ever. When you get your Free Books, if you don't want any more, just write cancel on the statement & return it to us.

★ You can of course go for prizes alone by not playing rows 4 & 5. But why pass up such good things? Why not go for all the prizes you can - & why not get everything that's being offered & that you're entitled to? It's all free, yours to keep & enjoy. It's a "SURE FIRE" opportunity for you!

"Yeah, but there are still all kinds of other things. All those reproductions of the mummy's rings and bracelets. Why would only the necklaces have sold out?"

We wandered back to the special Egyptian section and made a closer inspection of the cases.

"May I help you with something?" a clerk asked from behind the counter.

I nodded, sliding my hand under the mummy beads. "This necklace is a reproduction from the Egyptian exhibit, and I'd like to get another."

The clerk looked at the beads curiously, then shook her head. "I don't think those could have come from here. We didn't have any beads."

I glanced at Rev, my pulse beginning to race.

"You're certain about that?" he asked the woman.

"Well...I'm only part-time. Maybe you should speak to the manager. I'll get her."

"Rev," I whispered as she started away, "if they didn't have any beads, then these *have* to be Princess Amonit's."

"Dammit, Marina, you're jumping to conclusions. They could be—"

"No! I'm not jumping at all. Professor Reinhardt recognized the design, remember? He said the people here must have copied it from the mummy's X rays."

"Yeah, you're right," Rev said. "But calm down. That clerk could have been wrong. Maybe they *do* have copies of the beads. Maybe they're stashed away someplace or—"

"They don't have copies," I interrupted, positive I was right. "Remember what Reinhardt said when he first saw these? I didn't think anything of it until now, but he said he didn't know they were having reproductions of the necklace made. He said it wasn't one of the items he and Ashton Crawly had discussed as a possibility."

The clerk arrived back with her boss in tow, a well-dressed middle-aged woman named Mavis Hoskins.

This time, I dug out a card and explained that Sherwin McNee Indemnity needed information about the reproductions because of the *real* jewelry that the missing mummy had been wearing.

Mrs. Hoskins glanced at my beads and shook her head, saying, "I'm afraid there's some confusion here. We didn't have a necklace among the reproductions."

"You're sure," I said.

"Oh, yes. I helped decide which things we should have copied."

"Would you mind telling us about that?" I said. "How you decided?"

"No, of course not. It was several months ago. As soon as we knew for certain we'd be mounting the exhibit. There were four of us involved. Do you want names?"

"Please."

"Well, aside from me, there was Mr. Crawly, the exhibit coordinator, his administrative assistant, Janet Koslovsky, and the woman who looked after public relations for the exhibit. Her name is Susan Dafoe."

"And how did you decide which items to go with?"

"Well, Mr. Crawly got pictures from the L.A. museum. We had close to a hundred possible items to choose from, and we based our choices on which would be the easiest to have copied and what we thought would sell best."

"And did Crawly have a picture of a necklace?" Rev asked.

Mavis Hoskins shook her head. "I'm positive he didn't. If he had, I'd have pushed for it, because necklaces sell well."

Rev and I exchanged glances. Our "shopping" trip had definitely been productive.

DETECTIVE BARBONI HAD BEEN lurking in the museum's foyer when we left the gift shop, so we'd quickly headed down to the parking garage.

Rev checked under his hood and felt along under the edge of the chassis and in the wheel wells, as if that had become as much a part of his regular routine as unlocking the car doors.

It was a good thing the Porsche was too low to the ground for anyone to crawl under it or Rev would have been on his back checking the entire undercarriage.

"So?" he said, climbing in beside me. "Where the hell are we at here?"

"We're at the fact that my beads are the real thing," I murmured, still barely able to believe it.

"I don't know," he said. "I'm sure there's got to be some other explanation. We're just not thinking of it."

"Maybe we're not thinking of it because it doesn't exist, Rev. Everything adds up to their being real. Reinhardt recognized the design, and there were never any copies made. And... and that means maybe the voice was real, too... doesn't it?"

"That's just too damned hard to believe," he muttered. "I've always thought anyone who said the dead could communicate with the living was either a crackpot or a charlatan."

"An awful lot of people believe it's possible," I said. And I was no longer certain they were wrong.

"How about having someone who knows what they're doing check out the beads? There have to be people right in the Donner who could tell us whether they're actually three thousand years old or not."

I fingered them uneasily, finally saying, "I'm not sure that's a good idea. If we showed them to anyone in the Donner, and they *are* Princess Amonit's, that would be the last we'd see of them. Whoever looked at them would feel they had to tell Ashton Crawly. And he'd tell the police. And they'd take them as evidence."

"And they'd want to know how the hell we got them," Rev muttered. "Maybe you're right. All we'd need is the cops deciding we're suspects."

"Right. And...oh, Rev, as bizarre as this sounds, I'm starting to feel that wearing them really *will* keep me safe. I mean, that's what the voice said. As long as I wear them, Princess Amonit can protect me."

Rev ran his hand through his hair.

"So I don't want to show them to *anyone*," I persisted. "With all the publicity there's been about the theft, even an expert not connected with the museum would realize what they were."

"Only *if* they're authentic."

"I want to keep them, Rev," I said firmly. "Keep wearing them. Not forever. I know I can't do that. But until the police catch whoever murdered Charlie."

"He's probably the same guy who sent me the damned beads, who tried to set me up."

"You *do* think they're Princess Amonit's, then."

"Hell, I don't know what to think. But you know what's got me worried?"

I could come up with at least three possibilities without even trying hard: Tweetie's vanishing from a locked apartment, the danger of someone trying to blow up the

Porsche, and the fact that getting involved with the mummy case claim had gotten Rev into far more than he'd bargained for.

Reluctant to voice any of my thoughts, I simply waited for him to go on.

"For all I know," he muttered, "somebody's going to try planting evidence linking me to Charlie's murder as well as to the theft."

I nodded, adding that as a fourth worry to my list.

"Look," he said, starting the car, "it's getting too late for you to bother going into Sherwin McNee. So why don't you come back to my place? If we brainstorm for a while, maybe we can figure out who the hell is behind all this."

"Maybe," I agreed.

I doubted it, though. The note on the letterhead meant our man was probably someone at the Donner. And until I'd had a chance to talk to people there, I didn't even know who most of the players were.

But Detective Barboni had banished us from the museum, and the idea of going to Rev's apartment with him had a lot more appeal than the thought of going to my own place. After all, a murderer was on the loose, a murderer who knew where I lived.

WE'D HAD PIZZA DELIVERED, rather than going out for dinner, and I'd discovered that the feeling I'd gotten yesterday had been bang on. Spending time alone with Revington York, in his apartment, had turned out to be dangerous as hell.

His dark leather couch was so comfortable that sitting on it felt positively sinful.

Or maybe it was his arms around me that was making me feel sinful.

Or the faint, luxurious scent of leather, mingled with the faint, intoxicating scent of Rev himself.

Or, most likely, it was the way he kept interrupting our brainstorming by kissing me. Actually, it hadn't turned into much of a brainstorming session at all. It was more of a heartstorming one.

Outside it was nearing twilight, and the only words to describe the view from his apartment's vantage point on Russian Hill were *utterly romantic*.

The floor-to-ceiling windows looked northeast across San Francisco Bay. The sun, setting behind us over the Pacific, had turned the Bay's water golden, its final rays tinting white sails yellow. Just visible to our far right, the entire length of the Bay Bridge, stretching lazily across to Oakland, was bathed in a pale glow.

"It's incredibly beautiful," I murmured.

"So are you," Rev whispered, kissing my neck.

He was exaggerating, of course, but I loved hearing him say it.

The only problem with the wonderful things he kept saying, and the wonderful things he kept doing, was that they'd prevented us from making much progress with the mummy case mystery. In large part, that was because brainstorming with Rev wasn't nearly as enjoyable as kissing him.

His kisses were the warmest, most sensuous I'd ever tasted. Cuddling against his broad chest made me feel safe and secure. And the way he caressed my back sent delicious little tingles of arousal through my entire body.

"Know what?" he murmured.

"What?"

"I think you should reconsider my suggestion about staying here until things get sorted out."

Easing back a little, I gazed at him, trying to remember what it could possibly have been about those Research file photos that had made me think he was anything other than gorgeous.

He had the deepest blue eyes in the world. And the most kissable mouth. And his eight-o'clock shadow was undoubtedly the sexiest addition to a face I'd ever seen.

I lightly trailed my hand down his cheek. That shadow was a little rough to the touch. And to the kiss. But it was so deliciously masculine it only added to the pleasure of both.

And his long hair... I wound some of it around my fingers and began drawing his mouth closer to mine again.

"Marina, I'm serious. Let's talk about the idea for a minute."

I stopped winding his hair. I'd gone from totally distrusting him to completely falling for him with lightning speed, but I'd always been extremely slow and cautious about falling all the way into bed. "You still mean on the pullout couch in the den?" I asked.

"If promising you a sofa bed is the only way you'll stay," he said, brushing his fingers gently across my mouth.

"Mmmmm...I just don't know if it would be a good idea."

"Marina, I'd feel a hell of a lot better knowing you're someplace safe, that nothing serious is going to happen to you."

His words made me smile. Whether or not this was someplace safe for me depended entirely on how we defined safe. And as far as nothing serious happening to me was concerned, the more kissing we did, the closer we were getting to something definitely serious happening.

But whatever was happening between us was happening too fast for me to be comfortable with.

I felt as if I'd stepped onto a merry-go-round on Monday morning. And then someone had thrown a switch and started it going at breakneck speed. Rev and I hadn't had the slightest chance to get to know each other.

Yet here I was, seriously considering staying with a man I knew absolutely nothing about except what I'd read in a Research file. And, I realized, glancing at him with a sudden rush of emotion, I wanted to know everything.

"Why are you smiling?" he murmured, leaning closer and nuzzling my ear.

Draping my arms loosely around his neck, I leaned back and gazed at him.

"Why?" he asked again, smiling a smile so sexy I almost gave up on conversation.

"Oh...I was just thinking...so many crazy things have been going on that they're all we ever talk about."

"And what do you want to talk about?" he whispered, his breath so enticingly warm I was growing less interested in talking by the second.

"You," I made myself say. "I don't know anything about you."

"There's nothing interesting to know," he said, caressing the back of my hand with his thumb.

"Sure there is. Tell me about your family." When we'd been searching for Tweetie, I'd noticed there wasn't a single photograph on view in the apartment."

"I don't have any family."

"None?"

"No one," he said, his eyes clearly saying he didn't want me to press.

I thought back to last night, when he'd taken me home and Mrs. Richey had intercepted us with her questions. "She'd drive me nuts," Rev had said. "I hate people asking me personal questions."

But surely he didn't consider me nothing more than *people*. I glanced away, my feelings hurt.

"Hey," he said gently, "don't look like that. I'm not trying to shut you out. It's just that there isn't anything particularly interesting about my past. And I really don't like talking about myself."

He brushed my hair back off my cheek and turned my face toward him again ... and that was when I saw it.

For a panicked moment my throat felt stuffed with cotton. When I finally managed a word it came out a croak.

"What?" Rev said, eyeing me anxiously. "What's the matter?"

"Don't move," I murmured. "But look over at the floor, below Tweetie's cage."

"Oh, God," he whispered when he did.

"What are we going to do?"

"Get the hell out of here. That's what. But move as slowly as you can."

It was at least a minute before I could make myself move at all.

I'd never been in the same room as a snake before...except in a zoo, with solid glass between us. And there was nothing but fifteen feet of marble floor between the couch and this one.

A cobra. Somehow, I knew it was a cobra. And that cobras have poisonous fangs, that their bites can be fatal. It might kill me. If I didn't die of fright first.

But there was something fascinating about it that kept me frozen on the couch.

It sat perfectly still, watching us, its dark, hooded head raised straight up, about sixteen inches from the floor.

It was hard to tell, the way it was curled around itself, but I guessed its yellowish brown body was about three or four feet long.

Slim, though, only about an inch thick. Slim enough, I thought, swallowing hard, to slither through the bars of a bird cage.

"Get going," Rev hissed at me. "Head for the door."

I forced myself to move. As slowly as possible, I pushed up off the couch and began inching across the living room, my eyes not leaving the snake.

Then Rev edged in front of me, between it and me, and I couldn't see it any longer. I kept edging toward the foyer, trying not to remember how incredibly fast I'd seen zoo snakes slither.

Despite the way my legs were threatening to give out on me, I made it across to the broad archway between the living room and foyer.

"That's it," Rev whispered, taking my hand and starting to back out of the room. "We're almost there. Just a few more steps."

We stopped at the door while he fumbled backward with the dead-bolt.

Just when I was sure he'd never get the door open he did, yanking me out into the hallway so hard he almost pulled my arm off.

He slammed the door shut behind us and sagged against the wall, wrapping his arms around me and pulling me tightly to him.

With my cheek resting against his chest, I could feel his heart was pounding at least as hard as mine.

"What now?" I whispered at last.

"Now we call the cops. Your friend, Barboni."

I glanced fearfully at the door, then up at Rev. "His card is in my purse. And my purse is in your living room."

Rev gave me a shaky grin. "Please don't say you want me to go back in and get it."

Chapter Nine

Rather than terrifying any neighbors by announcing a deadly snake was loose in the building, we'd hurried down to the parking garage and used Rev's car phone to call the police. Fortunately, he'd had the presence of mind to grab his keys from the foyer table on the way by.

The operator put us through to a central police number, and someone there connected us with Barboni's division headquarters. As he'd promised, they knew how to get hold of him.

He called back within ten minutes, and it was less than an hour before the police had a herpetologist from the San Francisco Zoo on hand. Half an hour after that, both the snake expert and the cobra were gone.

The zoo has a fund-raising Adopt an Animal program, and I intended to call with a pledge in the morning. I hadn't yet decided what kind of animal I'd adopt, but it was going to be something warm-blooded that didn't bite.

Once the cobra had been removed, two of the police officers who'd arrived had searched Rev's apartment for anything else suspicious. They'd given it a clean bill

of health, and now only Frank Barboni and Lisa Rashkin were still with us.

It wasn't their normal shift, but they were working
overtime on Charlie's murder and clearly thought what
had been going on here was somehow connected.

I didn't find that reassuring, even though I hadn't
actually believed the snake had crawled into the apartment through a duct or anything like that.

There was no sign of forced entry, and Rev still insisted he'd never given anyone a key. But there was no
doubt someone had been in his apartment. He'd already called a twenty-four-hour locksmith to come and
replace his locks.

"So this story you read about the tomb in Egypt?"
Barboni said to me after he'd finished one of his whispered conferences with Rashkin. "About the cobra
eating the canary? Is it like folklore? I mean, something a lot of people would know about or not?"

"It wasn't folklore," I explained. "It really happened to the archaeologist who discovered King Tut's
tomb. Someone put a cobra in it, hoping to kill him. But
all it killed was his canary."

I glanced over at Tweetie's empty cage, feeling badly
and deciding that when I phoned in my pledge to the
zoo, I'd tell them I wanted to adopt a bird.

"It's a story millions of people must have heard,"
Rev said. "When Marina first mentioned it, I vaguely
recalled reading about it years ago. And I'm sure it's
been used in a few movies."

"I think I even saw something like it on 'Quantum
Leap,'" Rashkin put in.

"Millions of people," Barboni muttered. "Which
probably includes every single person who had any-

thing to do with the Donner's Egyptian exhibit. And it was yesterday your canary disappeared?"

Rev nodded. "Marina and I were in L.A. all day. He was here when I left in the morning and gone when we got back."

"And you're sure the cage door was closed."

"Positive."

"I wonder if that snake was in the apartment with you all last night?" Rashkin mused.

Rev's face paled a little.

"I don't think the snake had anything to do with the canary disappearing," Barboni said. "I think it's more likely we're dealing with somebody who has a black sense of humor. And if they came in here once they could have come in twice. Taken the bird yesterday, then brought the snake in today."

"But who?" I knew I wouldn't get a definite answer, but hoped Barboni at least had some suspicions he'd share.

No such luck. He merely shrugged, then turned his attention to Rev. "The uniforms talked to all your neighbors. All the ones who were home, at least. None of them noticed a stranger around here in the last day or two."

"Most of them are at work all day," Rev said.

Barboni nodded. As if it were a signal, Rashkin snapped her notebook shut.

"I did ask my CO about giving you some protection," Barboni told me as he stood up. "But I'm afraid it was a no go."

"What do you think about Marina staying alone in her apartment?" Rev demanded.

"I sure wouldn't," Rashkin said. "I'd rather check into the Bates Motel and worry about a psycho than stay where a murderer was expecting me to be."

Rev shot me an I-told-you-so look and said, "That's what I figured."

"I'd be careful in this place, too," Barboni told him. "I don't know what the hell is going on, but somebody obviously knows you've gotten involved in Sherwin McNee's investigation. And he doesn't like it."

"It should be safe enough in here once I've got the locks changed."

"Yeah ... should be. And the uniforms warned your neighbors to be extra careful about buzzing people into the building. Of course, whoever has a key to your apartment likely has one for the front entrance, too."

Rev swore, then said, "The president of our owners' association lives right next door. I'll go talk to him about having the main lock changed, too. It makes sense to do it tonight, while the locksmith's here, anyway. We'll just have to make sure we get new keys to everyone."

We saw the two detectives out. Then Rev closed the door, clicked the deadbolt into place, and turned to me with a silent question.

After Rashkin's *Psycho* remark, I didn't feel I had much choice as far as my answer was concerned. "I don't have anything here with me," I said.

"We can go by your place in the morning and get some of your things," Rev said. "For tonight, I'll lend you a T-shirt to sleep in. And there's a drugstore nearby that delivers. I'll get them to send over a toothbrush. Anything else you need that I might not have?"

I shook my head, for once not minding even a little that Rev had gone into his take-charge mode. I was too busy worrying about what our murderer might have up his sleeve next.

REV HAD BARELY finished talking to his next-door neighbor about replacing the main lock when the locksmith arrived.

He spent half an hour changing the locks, then told us it was going to take him at least that long to cut new front door keys for everyone—even though there are only four apartments on each of the three floors. It was a good thing the condo wasn't a high rise.

When the first of the new keys was cut, Rev and his neighbor went off to deliver them and briefly explain the problem. I went into the den and called my parents.

It turned out to be a wise move. My mother had heard about Charlie's murder on the noon news and had been frantically trying to get hold of me since then.

"When you weren't either at work or at home, I was worried sick," she said. "I must have left four messages on your machine. Or was it five? Did you count them?"

"No," I said, not correcting her assumption that I was calling from my own apartment. "I wasn't in the office all day, Mom. You know I'm out following up on claims most of the time."

"I know, dear, but why didn't you call me as soon as you heard what had happened?"

"Ahh . . . it didn't occur to me you'd be worried." I anxiously twisted the phone cord around my hand, wishing I knew exactly what the news coverage had said. If it had mentioned a possible connection between the car bomb and the mummy case claim, and my mother asked me precisely what I was working on at the moment . . .

"Well, your father and I *were* worried, dear. I almost died when I heard the announcer say the victim's name was Charles Obregon. They don't think it had anything to do with Sherwin McNee Indemnity, do they?"

I began breathing a little more easily. "I don't really know what they think," I said. Not exactly a lie. "But, look, I wanted to let you know I might be away for a few days. So you wouldn't call my apartment and wonder why I wasn't there."

"Oh? You have to go to L.A. again?"

"Maybe." Not *exactly* a lie, either. It might be unlikely, but it *was* a possibility.

"Well, do be careful, Marina. Ever since you told me you were there, I keep thinking how dangerous that city can be."

"I'll be careful. And I'll call you as soon as I'm back home. Give my love to Dad."

I hung up, thinking how dangerous *my own* city could be. Then, needing to talk to someone who would understand what was going on in my head, I called San Francisco General and asked for Nat Fishbein's room.

I'd have to test the waters carefully, of course. If Nat didn't know about Charlie, I wasn't going to risk getting him excited by telling him.

This time, there was no problem in being put through to his room. And it took all of five seconds for me to realize I didn't have to worry about testing the waters.

"What the hell is happening?" he practically hollered when I said hello. "I'm gone for a couple of days and Special Claims falls apart. Or gets blown up, I guess I should say."

"Not the entire department, Nat. Only poor Charlie. And you've been gone more than a couple of days. But I take it you saw the news?"

"News, schmooze. Those reporters didn't know diddly. But I talked to Homer Leibranch. *Poor Charlie* is right. What a *shmutsik* way to go. And Homer says you were helping out on that claim."

"Right, I was...*am,* Nat. Except that there's no one to help out anymore. There's only me at the moment."

"Hell, you're not ready for that sort of thing, Marina. Tell me exactly what's been happening and maybe I can help you."

"Nat, are you sure you should be worrying about this?"

"Worrying, schmorrying. I'm fine. They can't find anything seriously wrong with me at all. They're not so sure I even *had* a heart attack anymore. Now they're talking angina, which ninety percent of men end up with sooner or later. If none of their fool tests show anything, I'm outta here in another day or two. So tell, already."

I took a deep breath, then told him everything—from the moment Charlie had nailed me on Monday morning until the events of ten minutes ago tonight.

I only left out two things. Seeing the bird with the human head in the L.A. museum case, and hearing Princess Amonit's silvery voice.

Nat Fishbein is the most pragmatic man I've ever met. Telling him I really believed I'd seen Princess Amonit's *ba* and heard her voice would give him fits. And even though he claimed to be fine, I wasn't about to give fits to a man lying in a hospital.

"Wow," he muttered when I was finished my story. "Wow, talk about getting your feet wet by diving into the deep end."

"So, where do I go from here, Nat?"

"Well, not back to your own apartment, that's for damned sure. This Rev sounds as if he's got a sensible head on his shoulders. But you're absolutely convinced he can't have been in on it?"

"I wasn't sure at first, but I am now. Aside from anything else, nobody in his right mind would let a deadly snake loose in his own apartment and then sit calmly on the couch with me and . . ."

I caught myself. There were actually *three* things I hadn't told Nat about.

But I hadn't caught myself soon enough because he jumped on my line, saying, "Sit calmly on the couch with you and do what?"

I swore silently. Nat had three daughters, and I'd realized weeks ago what they must have gone through growing up with him as their father. If he'd been Catholic, he'd probably have had them raised in a convent.

"Rev and I were sitting on the couch brainstorming when we saw the snake. Just sitting trying to figure things out."

"Yeah? How old's this guy, Marina?"

"Oh . . . early thirties."

"And what's he look like?"

"He's okay-looking, I guess."

"Yeah? Well you just remember you've only known him for a few days. And make damned sure he hasn't got more on his mind than giving you a safe place to stay."

"All right, I will, Nat." Lord, telling my *own* father where I intended to spend the night wouldn't have gotten me a sterner warning.

"Be sure you do. And sleep with your gun under your pillow, just in case."

"All right, I will," I said again, even though I didn't know whether Nat was thinking about me using the gun against the murderer or Rev. "But where do I go from here as far as the claim is concerned?"

"You're sure you don't want off it?"

"As sure as I can be, I guess. I mean, I've decided I'd feel better trying to figure out what's going on than I would sitting around like a scaredy-cat. Especially knowing someone will probably have another go at killing me either way."

Nat was silent for a minute, then slowly said, "Well, it sounds to me as if you're right about your man working at the Donner. So all you can do is pick up where Charlie left off and see what you can find out there. Start at the top, with that guy you said did all the planning."

"Ashton Crawly, the exhibit coordinator."

"Right. Start with him. That way, you'll get an overall picture. Then work your way down through the ranks to fill in the details. And what about Revington York? You're sure he intends to keep helping out?"

"I don't think I could stop him, Nat. Not now that he figures someone was trying to set him up with the necklace. And especially not after the snake. It could have killed him."

"Or you," Nat muttered.

"Or me. But nobody knew I'd be here, so it must have been meant for him."

"Well, if he really does want to help, he should probably get his friend at the Donner involved. What did you say the guy's name was?"

"Scott Usher."

"And what's his job?"

"He's an assistant curator." I'd asked Rev that very question over lunch. "He works on mounting exhibits and does research. Things like that."

"Yeah? Well, tell Rev I suggested he be seen around the museum with the guy. It'll make people more likely to open up than they would to a total stranger."

"Okay, I'll tell him."

"And you be careful, Marina. Very careful."

"I will." I sure wished everyone would stop telling me that, though. They were only making me more nervous.

"And call me again tomorrow, huh? Let me know what's happening?"

"I will, Nat. Thanks for listening. And for the advice."

"Hell, I only wish I was in on this one, Marina."

"Not as much as I do, Nat."

I'd barely hung up when I heard the apartment door open and close. A minute later, Rev was standing in the den's doorway.

"I was just talking to Nat Fishbein," I said.

"And?"

Briefly, I repeated Nat's advice about how we should proceed. "And he suggested you get Scott Usher involved," I concluded. "Let people at the museum see the two of you together and make it obvious you're good friends."

Rev rubbed his jaw, not looking happy at the suggestion.

"What?"

"Well... Scott had nothing at all to do with the Egyptian exhibit. I remember Rachel mentioning that when all the excitement erupted."

"I don't think it matters, Rev. Nat's point was that if people saw you were a good friend of Scott's, they'd talk to you more freely."

"Yeah," Rev muttered, "I'm just not sure how Scott would react to the idea of getting involved."

"But he'd want to help a friend, wouldn't he?"

"Well, the thing is that we're actually not much more than acquaintances. I've transported things for the Donner in the past, and he was my liaison once. That, and his asking me to interview Rachel, is about the extent of things."

"But you said *good friends* when he phoned to tell you about Charlie asking questions. I remember distinctly."

"Yeah... well, that was to make you think he was telling me a lot more than he actually did."

I glared at Rev in annoyance. We needed all the help we could get.

"Don't look at me like that," he muttered. "I'll ask him. And he'll probably go along with it. I think he still figures he owes me for giving Rachel the job. That's probably why he called about Charlie in the first place.

"By the way," he went on after a minute, "I had these cut for you."

He tossed two new keys on the end of the sofa. "The one with the square end is for the front door. The other's for the apartment."

"I don't need them, Rev. I won't be here without you."

"Take them."

I took them, not knowing what else to do.

He continued to stand in the doorway, and the silence quickly grew awkward.

It was getting late. And I had a pretty good idea what he was thinking about because I was thinking about it, too. But I certainly didn't intend to act on my thoughts.

Horrifying as seeing the snake had been, its interruption had been timely.

Kissing Revington York wasn't conducive to rational thought. Quite the opposite. Kissing him slowed down my brain and sent my hormones into a frenzy.

At twenty-eight, I'm not entirely naive. But I'd never experienced such a powerful reaction to a man before. And I wasn't sure Rev was a man I should let myself react to.

I doubted he had a deep, dark, secret past, but the way he'd clammed up so tightly about himself earlier had hinted there were things he didn't want revealed. After all, most men love to talk about themselves.

Revington York, of course, wasn't *most* men. But stepping back a bit, until I was able to get a clearer perspective on what he really *was*, made a lot of sense.

As Nat had reminded me, I'd only known Rev for a few days. It could be that the unexpected intensity of those days had caused the unexpected intensity of my feelings for him.

And if that was the case, I didn't want to find I'd rushed into something I'd regret once we were out of this bizarre situation we'd been thrown into.

"Do you want me to pull out that couch for you?" Rev said at last.

I simply nodded, not trusting my voice to say yes, even though that's what my brain was ordering it to say. He was so darned gorgeous—all broad shoulders, lean height and dark good looks—that I couldn't stop thinking how warm and safe I felt in his arms. How delicious his lips were on mine. How delightfully teasing his tongue was. How being close to him made my bones melt and my common sense evaporate.

"You don't want to watch a little TV or anything?" Rev asked.

"No...no TV." I knew from looking for Tweetie that the only television set was in the bedroom. "I think we should both get a good night's sleep, Rev."

He gazed at me uncertainly, maybe trying to decide if I was playing hard to get.

"I'm really exhausted," I added. "You must be, too."

"Not *that* exhausted," he said, his expression more leer than grin.

"Ahh...Rev, about earlier...and with my staying here..." I could feel my face growing hot, but I didn't want any confusion about my message.

"I hope I haven't given you the wrong impression," I rushed on. "I...well, despite what I might have made you think, I like to take things slowly, okay?"

He pressed his lips together, then shrugged, saying, "I'll get you a T-shirt...and a robe. You can use the bathroom to change while I make up the couch."

I started to say I'd help, then thought better of it. Making up a bed with Rev wouldn't be one of my all-time smartest moves. Simply looking at him made my heartbeat quicken, let alone looking at him across a bed.

I TOOK TWICE AS LONG as necessary getting ready for bed, reluctant to go trotting down the hall from the bathroom with every stitch of my clothes draped over my arm.

Rev's T-shirt came halfway down my thighs and his robe practically reached my ankles, but we'd both know I was naked beneath them.

When I finally opened the bathroom door I was still feeling incredibly ill at ease.

The way Rev was hovering outside the den didn't help in the least.

We'd done a fair amount of kissing today, so it would seem strange not to kiss him good-night. But kissing him was like eating macadamia nuts. Almost impossible to stop after one. Of course, kissing him was a million times more enjoyable than eating macadamia nuts.

He shoved his hands into the pockets of his jeans and gave me a slightly crooked smile that said he felt the same awkwardness I did.

We needed a funny line or something to break the tension, but I was drawing a complete blank in the sense of humor department.

"I thought maybe you'd like something before you went to bed," he offered. "Coffee? Tea?"

He waited a few beats, then gave me a second crooked smile. "I hope you noticed that I didn't say, 'Coffee, tea or me.'"

I laughed quietly, feeling a little better. "I noticed. And thanks, but I don't want anything."

That was an outright lie, I thought, gazing into the blue depth of his eyes.

"Well...'night, then," he said.

"'Night, Rev."

He leaned forward and gently brushed his lips against mine. Even that was enough to start my blood scurrying faster.

"See you in the morning," he added, backing along the hall to his bedroom.

I closed the den door behind me, glancing to see if there was a lock on it.

There wasn't, but that didn't surprise me. And it didn't worry me. At least, I wasn't worried about Rev coming in and trying to ravish me in the night.

But that murderer...well, with Barboni and Rashkin figuring the snake was somehow connected to Charlie's murder, how could I think otherwise? And if the murderer knew where Rev lived...of course there were new locks on the doors...but still...

I could practically hear Nat's voice again, saying, "Sleep with your gun under your pillow, Marina, just in case."

I opened my bag, unzipped the compartment that held my .38, and carefully took it out.

My snubby, as Nat called it. He carried a semiautomatic pistol, but I hadn't had a clue about guns before I'd joined Special Claims, so I'd simply taken a standard issue Smith and Wesson revolver. Well, almost standard. Charlie had advised me to ask for a snubnose. He'd said most women preferred the two-inch barrel to the normal four inches.

But I'd gotten a shock when I'd discovered revolvers don't have safeties. I'd assumed all handguns had them, not just pistols. That's why I'd bought a bag with a special compartment. It took a serious squeeze to pull the trigger, and my shooting instructor said guns rarely got accidentally discharged, but I wasn't about to take a chance on anything in my purse getting tangled up with my gun.

I wasn't about to take a chance on it getting tangled up in a pillowcase, either, so I put it into the drawer of the bedside table.

Then I crawled under the blankets, switched off the lamp and lay waiting for sleep to come. And trying not to think about the mysterious Revington York, lying in the very next room.

Chapter Ten

I woke with a start, thinking for a frantic second I was hearing the rat-a-tat of a machine gun.

Then Rev said, "Marina?" and reality began clicking in.

The dark of night had been replaced by the pale gray of morning fog. And Rev was in the hall outside the den, knocking on the door.

Incredibly, I'd made it through till morning without a single nightmare. No images had terrified me while I slept. No mummies, no murderers, no snakes, no things that go bump in the night. Sleeping at Rev's was as effective as not eating dill pickles.

"Marina?" he said again, a little louder this time.

"Yes, I'm awake."

"I thought I'd make breakfast before we go over to get your clothes. What would you like?"

"Just coffee, thanks."

"Okay. Have a shower or whatever. It's not even seven-thirty, so there's no rush."

By the time I'd collected yesterday's clothes from the chair and headed for the bathroom, I could hear Rev in the kitchen. His not waiting to say good morning face-to-face had to be a sign that he'd bought last night's go-slow message.

My brain was relieved. My libido was saying a good morning kiss would have been a great way to start the day.

While I showered, my brain gave my libido a lengthy lecture on self-control. Working with Rev would be far less complicated if I kept the relationship platonic.

Then, after the mummy case claim was history, we could figure out if there really was something serious happening between us. Assuming, of course, neither of us ended up dead in the meantime.

That thought made me shiver, despite the heat of the shower.

We took our time over coffee, Rev being a perfect host and also a perfect gentleman. And in the clear light of day, the thought of his having a deep, dark, secret past seemed absurd.

After breakfast, we headed over to North Beach to pick up my things. I was just unlocking the front door of the building when Mrs. Richey popped out of her apartment.

"Good morning, dear...Mr. York," she said, beaming a knowing smile at us. I felt like a teenager who'd been nailed trying to sneak in after curfew.

"Good morning, Mrs. Richey," I said, aware my face was beet red.

Rev made a few innocuous comments to her about the weather, all the while navigating me past her to the stairs.

By the time we made it to the third floor, my face had stopped burning. Then a sudden queasy feeling hit me just outside my apartment door.

"Nervous?" Rev said.

When I nodded, he took the key and unlocked the door.

I held my breath as he opened it, but everything looked fine inside.

The light on my answering machine was blinking, so I switched it to play and listened to the five messages my mother had left yesterday. Each one sounded slightly more hysterical than its predecessor.

"I thought you were joking about their not believing you'd grown up," Rev said.

His amazed expression made me laugh.

"I told you," I said. "It's part of the only-child syndrome. As far as I can tell, my twelfth birthday was the last one that registered with them."

Rev smiled, a warm, sexy smile that seriously threatened my go-slow policy.

"I'll just change and get my things," I said, edging away from him.

He looked a little disappointed. Or annoyed. I couldn't tell which. But all he said was, "I'll phone Rachel while I'm waiting. Make sure she knows I'll be at the Donner if anything important comes up."

I changed into fresh clothes, packed a few outfits, then checked the time. It was getting close to nine, so I called Sherwin McNee, hoping Homer Leibranch was already in his office.

He was, and he sounded relieved to hear I'd gotten advice from Nat.

"Okay," he said once I'd filled him in. "Starting with this Ashton Crawly who coordinated everything makes sense. And having Revington York along might be just as well, because I can't put anyone else on that claim as fast as I'd wanted. Charlie was juggling more major investigations than I realized, and there isn't a single one

we can just leave hanging. Ahh . . . by the way, his funeral is tomorrow. Two o'clock at O'Conner's Funeral
Home, over on Fourth. We'll be closing the office at
noon.''

I swallowed hard, then said I'd either phone again or
go into the office before that.

"Fine. But look, why don't I give the Donner's director a call and pave the way for you a little? His name
is Griston, and I can at least explain to him why
Revington York will be with you.''

I managed to concentrate on the rest of what Leibranch had to say, but by the time I hung up I was
blinking back tears. All I could think about was Charlie's funeral. And that a bomb wouldn't have left much
to bury.

"What's the matter?'' Rev asked.

"Charlie,'' I murmured. "The funeral's tomorrow...I...maybe I should go and find something black
to wear...or, I don't know. I guess I can come back here
again. . . .''

Before I'd even realized he was moving closer, Rev
wrapped his arms around me and held me against the
warmth of his chest. Nothing more. Simply a consol-
ing hug. It meant a lot to me.

REV AND I CHECKED IN with Mr. Griston, the Donner's director, as soon as we arrived at the museum, and
he went out of his way to start us off on the right foot.
He even had a list of everyone involved in mounting the
Egyptian exhibit ready for us, both their names and
positions.

A quick glance told me Scott Usher's name wasn't on
it. I'd been hoping Rev had been wrong about Scott not
having had anything to do with it, but no such luck.

There were twelve names, only four of which I recognized: Ashton Crawly, Mavis Hoskins, the gift shop manager we'd spoken to yesterday, and the two other women she'd told us had been in on deciding which items would be reproduced to sell. Janet Koslovsky, Crawly's assistant, and Susan Dafoe from public relations.

"You two ask around all you like," Griston was saying. "If anyone objects, have them call me. I'll tell them you're to get complete cooperation."

While Griston was helpfulness personified, Ashton Crawly was the extreme opposite.

The initial pleasantries I tried, when we first got to his office, failed miserably. All he gave me in return were bad vibes. After a few minutes, the air was alive with them.

The sooner we got down to business, I told myself, the sooner Rev and I could move on to someone less hostile. "Maybe you could start," I suggested to Crawly, "by telling us step-by-step exactly what happened to the Egyptian pieces after they arrived."

"I've already done that for the police."

"I realize that. But if you wouldn't mind . . . ?"

He obviously minded a whole lot, so I decided it might be best not to push him. I didn't say another word and neither did Rev. We simply sat across the desk from the man, letting him take his time about beginning.

Crawly was a tall, skinny, storklike man whose suit probably looked better on a hanger than on him. He had a beaky nose and dull brown hair. His blue eyes were rheumy, and even though he couldn't be more than in his mid-forties, his face had wizened into permanent lines of malcontent. His pasty skin hinted that he never emerged from the museum into the sunlight. I kept catching myself trying to get a good look at his incisors and wondering if he took afternoon naps in a coffin.

"All right," he said at last, combining a patronizing smile with a loud sigh, as if he were about to do us the biggest favor in the world. "I'll start with when the crates arrived from L.A. Each of them was numbered and its contents itemized. Everything that was supposed to be shipped was delivered... at least, everything or a *replica* of it."

"That's what you figure?" Rev snapped. "That it was the phony my men delivered?"

Crawly leaned forward across his desk and eyed us with undisguised irritation.

Without conscious thought, my hand moved to my neck. It was Crawly getting closer...well, actually, it was his teeth getting closer, that bothered me.

I forced my hand down to my mummy beads. As usual, touching them made me feel less anxious.

Then I noticed Crawly was staring at them. I immediately felt anxious again. I should have thought to tuck them out of sight while we were in the Donner. Lord, I'd been so upset I wasn't thinking about half the things I should be, and it was too late to hide them now.

Crawly's face seemed to have lost color, but it had been so white to begin with that I might have only fantasized he'd turned an even whiter shade of pale.

"Yes," Crawly finally said in answer to Rev's question.

It had taken him so long, though, that I'd forgotten what the question had been. But Crawly's elaboration on his "yes" reminded me.

"I think," he said, "the police are dead wrong about the switch being made *after* the exhibit items reached the Donner. I think the cases were exchanged before they ever got here.''

Beside me, Rev's knuckles grew white on the arms of his chair. ''You mean exchanged before the exhibit left the L.A. museum? Or while they were in transit?''

''Professor Heinrich Reinhardt,'' Crawly said, ''would never have allowed anything to happen to the mummy case while it was in his museum. Therefore...''

I could see Rev's face taking on that ''about to come over the desk'' expression he'd treated me to the first time I'd met him, so I quickly said, ''Exactly what makes you sure the switch couldn't have been made here at the Donner?''

''Because to get the reproduction in, and the genuine case out, would have meant getting them through shipping and receiving without anyone's knowing. And our controls are too tight for that to have happened.''

''You're positive?'' I asked.

''Yes. There's a receiving form for everything that comes into the building and an authorization form for everything that goes out. I personally sign the authorization forms for exhibit items.''

''What about after hours?'' Rev said. ''When nobody's here?''

''There's never nobody here. Security guards do rounds all night.''

''Then maybe somebody figured a way around having the proper paperwork,'' Rev said.

Crawly shook his head. ''As I said, *everything* that moves through shipping requires an accompanying form. And our forms are consecutively numbered, so each one is easily accounted for. Only one mummy case came in. And none went out.''

I made a mental note to check the records at some point, but I doubted I'd find anything out of order. Whoever had planned this was too smart to leave a paper trail.

"Well, maybe the cases didn't go through the shipping area, then," Rev was saying. "But they could have been taken in and out some other way."

"There isn't any other way," Crawly said. "Crated, the cases would have been far too big to get through any doors except shipping's."

"How about uncrated?" I asked.

"What do you think? That some weight lifter tucked a five-foot mummy case under his coat and waltzed out the front door with it? Or any of the other doors, for that matter?"

"There's no need to be sarcastic," Rev snapped. "Ms. Haine has to consider every possibility."

I flashed him a tiny smile of thanks for sticking up for me.

Crawly gave him a glare and said, "The regular doors *aren't* a possibility. When the museum is open, there's a guard posted at every exit. After hours, the security alarm is activated.

"So," he went on, "do you want me to get back to what happened after the pieces were delivered, or shall I give you a more detailed discourse on our security system?"

I ignored the fresh sarcasm and said, "We'll be talking to the security people themselves. So why don't you stick to the exhibit pieces?"

"All right. The crates were taken to a climatization room. They were opened, the contents were checked, and my staff wrote condition reports."

Rev picked up on that faster than I did, saying, "And whoever wrote the condition report on the mummy case took it to be the genuine item? One of the museum staff examined it and didn't even suspect it was a forgery? Yet *you're* positive it was a forgery that my men delivered?"

"It was an excellent reproduction," Crawly said coldly. "And we weren't checking for authenticity. Merely condition."

Rev looked so steamed I expected him to explode, but he merely shrugged at me. Apparently, he felt the same way I did. We weren't going to get anything useful from Crawly.

"Well," I said, "thank you for your time, Mr. Crawly." I knew I should have thanked him for his *help*, but the word would have stuck in my throat.

"We'll let you get back to work now," I added, standing up. "We still have to talk to everyone else who worked on mounting the exhibit."

He seemed about to object, so I quickly said, "Mr. Griston gave us permission to do that. But we won't take any more of your time."

"Not at the moment, at least," Rev added.

"What do you think?" I murmured to him once we were out of earshot of Crawly's office.

"I think the guy's a first-class jerk," he muttered.

"Me, too. I wouldn't give two cents for Crawly's theories."

"I wouldn't, either. And why would he be so damned defensive if he didn't have something to hide? I think he could be our man."

"I don't know, Rev. I'd love him to be the one, but it seems too easy. Too obvious."

"Maybe he was counting on people thinking that. But he *is* the one who authorizes everything that comes and goes. So assuming the switch *was* somehow made through the shipping area..."

"But if it wasn't...you know, for all he pooh-poohed the idea, the mummy cases *would* have fit through the regular doors uncrated. So maybe at night...?"

"It's a possibility," Rev said. "I'll bet somebody good enough could bridge just about any alarm system. And even during the day, if one of the guards was paid off...or if one of the shipping guys was involved..."

"Look," I said, "why don't I phone Barboni and see what he'll tell us? They'll already have questioned the guards and everyone in shipping."

We headed for the pay phones in the museum foyer, and I dialed Barboni's number.

He and Rashkin were off duty, which I realized I should have expected after their double shift yesterday.

"Is it an emergency?" the officer who'd taken my call asked after I gave her my name. "He left word we were to reach him for you if it is."

"No, no emergency. But would you leave him a message to call me, please? I'll be at the Donner most of the day, and he can get me later at Revington York's number."

"So, where do we go from here?" Rev said when I hung up.

"Think we should talk to Scott Usher before we hit anyone else on our list? See what he can do to smooth the way for us?"

"Yeah...I guess. I just hope he doesn't figure I'm asking him to risk his life by being seen with us."

I shot him a quizzical glance.

"You know. The bomb in your car. Then the snake. People say things come in threes."

"I don't believe in that sort of nonsense," I said firmly.

Of course, I reflected as we started for Scott Usher's office, I never used to believe in *ba*s or spirits' voices, either.

EVEN THOUGH REV HAD SAID he and Scott Usher were acquaintances, rather than friends, Scott couldn't have been friendlier. Or more accommodating.

"Absolutely," he said. "If Griston wants you to have complete cooperation, nobody will say a word if I spend the entire day showing you around. You want to see the Egyptian exhibit before we start on that list of names? It might give you a better idea of what to ask people."

When we said that sounded like a good idea, Scott took us to the gallery it was mounted in.

While we walked, I tried to imagine him and Rachel Windsor as a couple.

They must have been together for quite a while, because Rev had said it was last year that Scott had asked him to interview Rachel.

And physically, they'd make an attractive pair. Her, slim, blond and beautiful. Him, about Rev's age and height, with curly brown hair and a build that suggested he might have played football in college.

But once I got beyond the physical, my mental picture of them together grew fuzzy. I hadn't liked Rachel. I don't take to women whose zillion-watt smiles are reserved strictly for men. And I suspected that underneath her smiles she was tough as nails.

Scott, on the other hand, seemed extremely easy-going. He was nodding greetings to almost every staff person we passed.

A perfect example of opposites attracting, I decided as we reached the exhibit.

Compared to the L.A. museum, with its entire Egyptian wing, the display on loan to the Donner seemed very small. It was nicely set up, but the empty space where the mummy case belonged was jarring.

The forgery had been withdrawn from view. In its place stood a placard which simply stated, "Item temporarily removed." As if anyone who read newspapers or watched the news wouldn't know what had been removed and why.

I stood gazing at the space for a minute. Despite myself, I half expected to see something flying inside the glass case. There was nothing, so I followed Rev and Scott along to look at the rest of the pieces.

When we'd seen everything, we paused at the archway that led from the Egyptian display to a permanent exhibit of Shoshone pottery.

"So, what's next?" Scott asked.

"Well," I said, "we should have a look at the shipping area, and check out the security measures. And we'll have to talk to everyone on Mr. Griston's list."

"Let me see who all is on it."

I handed it over, and Scott quickly read through the names, then passed it back to me.

"The only person we've talked to so far is Ashton Crawly," Rev said. "And if everybody else is as uncooperative as him, we're in big trouble."

"Yeah . . . well . . ." Scott muttered, straightening his already-straight tie.

"You think he had a reason for not telling us much?" Rev asked. "He was damned defensive."

"Nah, I doubt it. That's the way he always is. The guy lives in Paranoid City."

"But maybe he has a specific reason to be paranoid about the exhibit?" Rev persisted.

"I don't think it's likely. Crawly's a pain in the butt, so you know how it is. People would really like him to have been involved with the switch. But I'm sure it's nothing more than talk."

"What's nothing more than talk?" I asked, a mental alert flashing in my head. Whatever the rumor mill had to say, I wanted to hear.

Scott shrugged. "I'm not much for repeating gossip, and the stuff about Crawly is really ridiculous."

Rev and I kept quiet, waiting until the silence prompted Scott to continue.

"Well . . ." he said at last, "I really *don't* like gossiping, but I know more than one person mentioned it to the cops, so somebody's bound to tell you, too. I guess it might as well be me. It's about Crawly and his administrative assistant. Her name's on your list. Janet Koslovsky."

When I nodded, Scott went on. "Crawly and Janet work very closely together. She probably does at least half his job. And she's one of the few people at the Donner who gets on well with him. In fact," he added, glancing around as if he'd be embarrassed at being overheard, "some people say they get on *really* well . . . if you know what I mean."

"You mean they're involved," Rev said bluntly.

"Yeah, at least that's the scuttlebutt. I don't believe it, though."

"Why not?" I asked.

"Well, first of all, because Janet has a boyfriend. One of the restorers, right here in the museum. He's a good buddy of mine. A hell of a nice guy, named Joe Callivetti."

I didn't think that name was on the list, but surreptitiously checked. Just as I'd thought, Joe Callivetti hadn't worked on the exhibit.

"So, since she's going with Joe," Scott continued, "why would she mess around with anyone else? Especially someone right under Joe's nose? Most especially Creepy Crawly?"

"Creepy Crawly?" I said, unable to keep from smiling.

Scott grinned again. "That's what everyone calls him. At any rate, *he's* what makes the idea of Janet cheating on Joe totally ludicrous. I mean, she's only in her late twenties, and not bad-looking."

I could certainly see Scott's point. I had a lot of trouble imagining *anyone* being involved with pasty-faced Ashton Crawly, let alone someone young and not bad-looking. But there was no accounting for taste. I didn't offer an opinion. Merely nodded encouragement to Scott and hoped his story was heading someplace even more interesting.

"You know," he said, gazing at me with a curious expression, "now that I think about it, Janet looks like you. I mean, you're better than not bad-looking," he added politely. "But she has long dark hair like yours. And bangs. And . . . well, she *does* look a lot like you."

I tried to smile. That was probably the appropriate response. But for some reason I didn't like the idea of this unknown Janet Koslovsky looking like me.

Maybe it was the thought that someone who looked like me might be having an affair with Creepy Crawly.

Or maybe it was that I already had one weird look-alike coincidence going, with the painted face on the mummy case.

"Anyway," Scott continued, fussing at his tie again, "the thing that's got everybody talking is that nobody's seen Janet for a while."

Idiot that I can be at times, I didn't catch his drift until he added, "So, they're all dying to know whose body was in the phony mummy case."

"Oh, my God," I whispered. The story had suddenly gotten a lot more interesting. And a lot more frightening to boot.

First, I'd discovered I looked like an ancient Egyptian princess had. And now I was learning I looked like a woman people suspected might be a mummified murder victim.

That was too much. I glanced at Rev, wondering if he'd noticed how the coincidences were piling up. Then I realized I'd never told him about my resemblance to Princess Amonit.

Rev wasn't paying any attention to me. He was eyeing Scott, saying, "And people think that maybe Crawly...? The police must be darned eager to get that body identified."

"From a few things they said, I'll bet they are. If it *is* Janet, then they could concentrate all their effort on that angle. But I hear that the body's being mummified has slowed down identification."

I nodded, recalling that Charlie had said something about the police having to go the dental ID route.

"At any rate," Scott went on, "what people around here think is that, square one, Crawly might well have had something to do with the mummy case caper. After all, he was in charge of the whole shooting match."

"So if anyone was in the perfect position to pull a switch it was him," Rev offered.

"Right. And if it *was* him ... well, like I said, he and Janet worked very closely together. So she might have known what he was up to. Or maybe she found out at some point. And anyone could have figured out how to mummify a body. An hour's research in the museum library would have done it."

"Oh, my God," I whispered again, unable to keep the words from slipping out.

Strangely enough, although I'd been able to imagine Crawly as a vampire, the thought that Rev and I might have just been sitting across a desk from a murderer completely threw me.

I started wondering if Crawly had noticed a resemblance between Janet and me ... and if that might have had anything to do with how hostile he'd been.

"Personally, I think everyone's way off base," Scott went on. "As I said, they don't like Crawly, so they'd just love it if he turned out to be an honest-to-God Jekyll and Hyde. But I figure the body came from a morgue. The woman was probably some Jane Doe murder victim the police hadn't identified."

"But this Janet Koslovsky," Rev said. "You say nobody's seen her lately?"

"No, not for a few weeks."

"And nobody knows where she is?" I added.

"Well, that depends. I mean, Crawly has a story that explains things ... kind of. But a lot of people don't believe it."

"And?" Rev said. "The story is ... ?"

"Well, see, Janet didn't show up for work a few Mondays ago. Three, I guess it would have been. And Crawly said she'd called him at home on the weekend and told him she had to take some time off work. According to him, she was really vague about the details, but one of her friends was someplace in the Caribbean and had run into trouble. And Janet was going down to bail her out. Nobody thought anything of it at first. No, I shouldn't say *nobody*," Scott corrected himself. "I remember talking to Joe Callivetti, and he was worried."

"That's her boyfriend. Who's a restorer here," I checked, wanting to make sure I had the players straight.

"Right."

"And she didn't call *him* to tell him where she was going?" Rev said. "But she *did* call Crawly?"

"Well, Crawly's her boss, don't forget. It made sense that she'd let him know she'd be away. And Joe was out of town the weekend this happened. Fishing in Oregon. Janet couldn't have reached him if she'd wanted to. But Joe had never heard anything about her having a friend in the Caribbean, so he thought the story was pretty strange. And then, when Janet never did contact him... well, I think it was a week or so later that he called the police."

"And?" I prompted.

"And apparently they weren't too concerned. They figured she was lying on a beach somewhere with her friend. But then, with this mummy case thing, when it came out that the mummy inside the reproduction was... fresh? Is that how you'd put it?"

I shuddered. That definitely wasn't how I'd put it.

"Anyway, that's why people can hardly wait until the mummy is identified," Scott concluded. "But like I said, I think they're way off base. Janet probably *is* lying on a beach with her friend."

"Marina?" Rev said. "You look sick."

"I *feel* sick," I murmured. Every time I started thinking about some woman being murdered and mummified, I got upset all over again.

"You want to get out of here?" Rev asked. "Come back and talk to people some other time?"

Uncertainly, I rested my hand on my mummy beads, half *hoping* I'd hear the silvery voice, half *afraid* I would.

I heard nothing. But I recalled, word for word, what it had said before.

"Do not give up," it had told me. "As long as you wear my beads, you are safe. I can help and protect you."

But was I really going to rely on the promise of protection from a princess who'd been dead three thousand years? After someone had killed Charlie? And murdered a woman who might not have been Janet Koslovsky, but had certainly been someone?

"Marina?" Rev said again.

"I'll be fine, Rev. Really, I'll be perfectly all right." I forced a smile, desperately wishing I felt more certain about that.

Chapter Eleven

"Could we stop by my apartment on the way to yours?" I asked Rev as he pulled out of the Donner's parking garage. "I really do need something to wear to the funeral tomorrow."

He nodded as I let myself melt into the luxury of the Porsche's leather seat. I was exhausted. Both mentally and physically. As much as I was dreading tomorrow, I was glad today was over.

We'd thoroughly checked out Shipping and Receiving, and had spent an hour touring the entire museum with its head of security. The systems and procedures, everywhere, appeared incredibly well organized and regulated.

If Barboni and Rashkin hadn't seemed so certain the switch had been made inside the museum, I doubted Rev and I would even still believe it was possible. But they were the *real* detectives. By comparison, we were rank amateurs.

In addition to the tours, we'd talked to six of the twelve people on our list.

Number seven, Janet Koslovsky, wasn't available to be talked to, since no one knew where she was.

The other five, the ones we'd left for tomorrow morning, included the electrician who'd done the exhibit lighting, two carpenters who'd readied the space, and the two men from maintenance who'd physically moved the display items from the climatization room to the gallery.

I doubted any of them would wind up on a suspect list. They'd all been only peripherally involved, and only toward the end of the exhibit preparations.

We drove in silence for a mile or two, then Rev looked over and said, "So, you're thinking it's got to be Crawly?"

"No... I was thinking about something else entirely. Something really strange."

He grinned at me. "You want to be more specific? An awful lot you think about seems really strange."

I tried to smile back but couldn't manage it, so I simply said, "Well, try this. Rev, I look like Princess Amonit. Honest," I insisted at his skeptical glance. "I realized it the first time I saw the photos of the mummy case. The resemblance struck me as eerie, but I chalked it up to coincidence. This morning, though, when Scott started in about my looking like Janet Koslovsky..."

Rev took his hand off the stick shift and rested it on mine. "Hey," he said quietly, "what Scott said doesn't mean a thing. He's probably one of those people who figures everybody he meets looks like someone he already knows."

"You think so?"

"I'm sure of it. He figures Rachel looks like Madonna."

I wrinkled my nose at that. Madonna was no California girl, and Rachel definitely was.

"And when he first met me," Rev went on, "he said I put him in mind of a cross between Clark Gable and Burt Reynolds. But better-looking than either of them, of course."

"Very funny," I said, feeling myself smile.

"Nobody else said anything about a resemblance, Marina. Not even Creepy Crawly. And surely he'd have noticed if there really was one."

"I guess." I considered mentioning that I'd thought a few of the others had eyed me strangely, even though they hadn't said anything, but decided to keep quiet.

There wasn't any point in making Rev decide I was any weirder than he already had to figure I was.

Besides, maybe nobody had looked at me strangely at all. Maybe my imagination had been working overtime.

"Hey," Rev said, "stop worrying. I'll bet Scott could as easily have decided you looked like Susan Dafoe as like Janet Koslovsky."

"Susan Dafoe? The PR woman?"

Rev shrugged. "She does kind of look like you."

I pictured Susan Dafoe. She *was* about my age, height and build. And her hair was only a little lighter brown than mine. I was beginning to feel awfully common, as if people might mistake every second woman in North America for me.

"Look, let's forget about what Scott thinks," Rev said. "Why don't we compare notes on the people we talked to? For starters, I figure we can rule out Mavis Hoskins."

"Me, too," I agreed. Aside from helping decide which items would sell best in her gift shop, she'd really had no involvement.

"And what about the PR ladies?"

I conjured up my mental picture of Susan Dafoe a second time, then added one of her assistant, whom I'd also met. They comprised the Donner's entire public relations department, and were typical of most PR people I've met. Bubbly personalities, wide smiles, and dying to help with anything and everything . . . or, at least, pretending they were.

"I'd rule them out, too," I said at last. "Except for the nagging detail of the note that came with the beads."

"It was just to throw me off track," Rev said. "I thought we managed to ask them some darned sneaky questions about that so-called thank-you gift. And the more they said, the more obvious it was that they didn't have a thing to do with sending the beads. Didn't you think so?"

"I guess . . . unless one of them was putting on an act."

"I doubt it. They weren't really involved much with the actual exhibit pieces, so I can't see what help they'd have been to our mastermind. Which gets us down to an awfully short list."

"You're writing off the guys we haven't talked to yet?"

"Pretty much. I'll be surprised if they say anything interesting. But how did you like the way Janet's two co-workers went to town on Crawly? Hell, I could hardly believe it. Especially not when he's their boss."

"And people say *women* are gossips," I teased. But I'd been amazed, too.

The two fellows had worked directly with Janet Koslovsky, doing the initial reports on the condition of the pieces, then designing the exhibit. And while the women we'd talked to had been circumspect, these guys had elaborated considerably on the story Scott Usher had told us.

If we were to believe them, Creepy Crawly and Janet Koslovsky had been having the most torrid affair since Marc Antony and Cleopatra.

Then, so their theory went, she'd discovered that he'd switched the mummy cases. When she'd threatened to call the cops, Ashton Crawly had murdered and mummified her. To cover his tracks, he'd concocted the explanation about her taking off for the Caribbean.

It all sounded too bizarre to be true. But the story of a modern mummy was already too bizarre. And it *was* true.

Still, the way I figured things, if the police had bought the theory they'd have Crawly under arrest by now. Which they didn't.

"I just don't know what to think," I finally said. "Maybe once Barboni gets back to us and fills us in on whatever he can, we'll be able to make more sense out of things. We need facts about Crawly, but all we have is conjecture."

"That's not quite all we have. We've got a missing woman and an unidentified body."

"Oh, Rev, did you have to say that? Thinking about a *fresh* mummy, as Scott so indelicately phrased it, has been giving me the creeps since day one. And now that we've heard so much about Janet Koslovsky...I almost feel as if I know her. So, if it does turn out to be her...it's crazy, but I don't want it to be. I want it to be someone whose name means nothing to me."

"Yeah, I know," he said. "But if it *does* turn out to be her, Crawly's our man."

Closing my eyes, I tried to stop thinking about the mummy case for at least a little while.

I'd expected my work in Special Claims to be interesting. I hadn't expected it would frighten the hell out of me. Or endanger my life.

Boring old Auto Claims was looking more and more like a place I'd rather be.

REV PULLED INTO the No Standing zone in front of my apartment and didn't even ask about coming up with me. He simply cut the engine and opened his door.

"Don't you ever get towed?" I asked.

"Nope," he said, grinning at me. "The cops might have one or two guys who know how to disarm the alarm, but none of the towing companies have figured it out yet. If they towed me, the noise would drive them crazy."

Just as she had this morning, Mrs. Richey appeared in the foyer before I even had the building's outside door unlocked. She stood peering anxiously through the glass at us.

"Jeez," Rev muttered, "I don't know why I ever worried about the security in your building. That woman's on duty twenty-four hours a day."

"Shhhh," I hissed, opening the door and saying hello to her.

"Hello, dear," she chirped. "I've been waiting and waiting for you."

"Oh?" Her comment unsettled me. Mrs. Richey looked like a kid who'd been caught with her hand in the cookie jar.

Well, actually, she looked like a little old lady who'd been caught with her hand in the cookie jar. But, whichever, I was sure it had been *my* cookie jar.

"What's up?" I prompted.

"Oh, nothing dear. Nothing at all. It's just that you didn't mention anyone was coming by today. And afterward, I started thinking perhaps I shouldn't have let her in. I'm certain it was all right, though, wasn't it? She said she'd only be a minute. And that's all she was. I waited right in the hall outside your door for her."

While Mrs. Richey was speaking, the unsettled feeling had been replaced by an icy chill, rapidly slithering up my backbone. "You let someone into my apartment?" I said, not quite able to keep a squeak out of my voice.

"Oh, my, I'm sorry, I didn't tell you who it was. I should have said straight away. It was your sister, dear. You know I'd never let a stranger in if you hadn't told me to expect someone. I promised you that when you gave me a key. But I was sure your sister would be fine. And I *did* offer to keep the present in my apartment until you got home, but she insisted she had to take it right upstairs herself. I think she wanted it to be a surprise for you. And now I've spoiled it, haven't I?"

"Which of her sisters?" Rev asked, sounding perfectly calm.

I glanced anxiously at him. He knew I was an only child.

"Oh, goodness," Mrs. Richey said, giving me a nervous smile. "Until today, I didn't know you even had *one* sister, let alone more than one, dear. You've never talked about your family."

"Which sister?" Rev asked again. "What was her name?"

"Why, it was Janet. Your sister Janet, Marina. And she looked so much like you, dear, I'd have known the two of you were sisters without her telling me. The same height, the same brown hair, why—"

"How big was this present?" Rev interrupted.

I was glad one of us could still speak, because *my* mouth felt dry as cotton balls.

"Oh, not big at all. Just the size of a teacup box. Seeing it took me back, I must say. When I was young, we always gave teacups as bridal shower gifts."

Mrs. Richey paused, glancing from me to Rev, then smiling broadly. "Oh, my, there isn't a bridal shower for you, is there Marina? You didn't get engaged and not tell me, did you?"

When I shook my head she looked disappointed. "Oh. Oh, I thought for a minute... it was so nicely wrapped, with a big bow and all. Is it your birthday, then, dear?"

I simply shook my head again, certain I wouldn't be able to answer if I tried.

"Well," Rev said, taking my arm. "Let's get upstairs and see what sister Janet left you."

He hustled me to the stairs before Mrs. Richey could say another word, then proceeded to mutter to himself the entire way up to the third floor.

By the time we reached my door, I thought I might be able to manage words.

"Janet?" I whispered. "As in Janet Koslovsky?"

"That would be the obvious guess. But what the hell is going on?"

My hands were shaking, so I handed the key to Rev.

He stuck it in the lock.

Then hesitated.

Then slowly moved his hand away from it.

"Get back," he ordered, glancing at me. "Get away from the door."

"What are you doing?" I demanded, not moving an inch. "You think there might have been a bomb in that box, don't you?"

"No... not really. It's just that after Charlie... and your car..."

"Rev," I said, grabbing his arm, "get away from that door!"

He rubbed his jaw, staring at the key in the lock, and finally said, "You're right. We'd better go back downstairs and phone Barboni."

We raced down to the foyer once more.

Mrs. Richey was still there.

"I didn't do something I shouldn't have, did I?" she asked with an anxious frown. "Is everything all right?"

"Don't worry," I told her. "Everything's fine." Unless, I silently added, the entire building blows up when my door gets opened.

I sat in the Porsche beside Rev while he plugged the car phone into the cigarette lighter, beeped in a code, then called Barboni. This time, the detective was in his office. Rev flicked the hands-free switch, so I could hear both sides of the conversation.

"Okay," Barboni said. "You did the right thing. Lisa Rashkin and I are on our way. You stay right in the car and wait for us. I'll get some guys from the bomb squad over there, too, just in case. If the package was that small, I don't think we'll have to worry about clearing the building. But if it *is* a bomb, it could make a hell of a mess of Marina's apartment."

"It must have been Janet Koslovsky," Rev said. "But does that make any sense to you?"

Barboni noisily cleared his throat, then said, "I'm pretty sure it wasn't Janet Koslovsky. So, while you're waiting, why don't the two of you try figuring out who else it might have been?"

Rev reached for my hand as Barboni broke the connection and gave it a hard squeeze, saying, "You heard him. He said, 'Just in case.' It's probably not a bomb at all."

"Sure," I murmured. "It's probably a teacup. For some reason, a strange woman dropped by and claimed to be my sister so she could put a teacup in my apartment."

"Right," Rev said with an abysmal attempt at a smile. "For some reason. We just don't know what it was."

I swallowed hard, not wanting to think about all my worldly possessions being blown away.

FRANK BARBONI and Lisa Rashkin arrived in an unmarked car, screeching up behind the Porsche three seconds before a cruiser did.

Two uniformed cops piled out of the front of it. While Barboni was introducing us to them, two officers who turned out to be with the bomb squad emerged from the back seat. The bomb squad truck would arrive shortly. The truck, I learned as the officers unloaded gear from the cruiser's trunk, was so heavy it was kept up on jacks, which meant it didn't have a fast response time.

Barboni must have filled the others in by phone or police radio, because they all knew the details of what had happened.

"We can do a preliminary check of your apartment before the truck gets here," one of the officers was saying to me. "We only need the truck if we *do* find explosives. We dismantle them inside it," he explained after a moment.

My face, I realized, had to look as blank as my mind felt.

"You don't think something could have been wired to the door?" Rev asked.

"Not if the woman was only inside the apartment for a minute."

"All right," Barboni was telling the two uniformed cops. "You question this Mrs. Richey. Get everything she can remember about the woman who delivered the package. Time, appearance, what she said. You know the drill.

"Lisa and I will come upstairs with you," he added, turning to the others. "You two wait downstairs," he told Rev and me.

"No, we need her," one of the men said, gesturing at me. "She's the only one who'd notice something out of place."

"If she's going up, so am I," Rev said.

Barboni simply shrugged, and we all headed into the building, the bomb squad fellows toting pieces of an outfit that looked like a brown canvas space suit.

Mrs. Richey eyed us as we came through the doorway, looking positively terrified.

"Everything is going to be okay, Mrs. Richey," I said, squeezing her hand. "These officers just want to ask you a few questions about the woman who was in my apartment."

"She wasn't your sister?" she murmured, her voice quavering.

"No, but I know you thought she was. So don't be nervous. Just tell them what you remember about her."

Poor Mrs. Richey didn't seem at all reassured, but when the officers introduced themselves very politely she seemed to relax a little.

Giving her what I hoped looked like an encouraging smile, I started for the stairs where Rev had waited for me. He took my hand and we headed up after the others.

My key was still in the lock where we'd left it, and my gaze kept returning to it as we stood waiting while one of the men put on the pieces of the space suit.

I couldn't stop wondering what would happen when he went into my apartment. If a bomb *did* explode, would that suit be enough protection?

It was thickly padded, and the chest protector was made of something like chain mail. The heavy helmet was like a welder's, with a clear, protective visor that flipped down in front of his face. By the time he was completely dressed, he looked like a brown Darth Vader.

He motioned the rest of us down to the end of the hall, then shuffled awkwardly to the door and fumbled at the key with his mitted hand.

I held my breath, reminding myself someone had said the woman wouldn't have had time to wire anything to the door.

Even with five of us standing in the hallway, it was so silent we heard the tiny click of the the key turning...followed by more silence that let me breathe again.

No bomb. At least not yet.

Cautiously, Darth Vader moved to the side of the door. He pressed himself against the wall, opened the door, then pushed it in. Only when it stood fully open, did he move away from the wall and go into the apartment.

Once inside, he seemed to have vanished forever. Then, just when I thought I was going to die from the tension, he reappeared in the doorway.

Balanced on one of his big mitts were the top and bottom of a teacup-sized gift box.

Without a word, the rest of us started down the hall toward him.

Rev had been holding my hand while we'd waited, and he gave it a reassuring squeeze. I tried to glance at him but couldn't force my eyes off the box.

The two pieces had been wrapped separately, so the cheery yellow gift wrap wasn't torn. And the big bow Mrs. Richey had mentioned was still attached to the lid. The box itself was completely empty.

"What do you think?" the officer who'd remained in the hall with us asked his buddy.

Darth flipped up the shield on his helmet and said, "The box was sitting open on the coffee table. I did a quick once-through and couldn't see anything planted. But if there *is*...maybe you'll spot something that's not right," he added, looking straight at me.

"I'll come in with her," Rev said.

"No," the bomb-squader told him. "Just her. The more people in there the more dangerous things get."

Rev muttered something under his breath, then gave my hand another squeeze and released it.

Darth moved aside.

I rested my fingers on my mummy beads, but even that wasn't enough to make me feel safe under the circumstances.

My entire body shaking, I stepped through the doorway. The word dangerous wouldn't stop echoing in my ears.

"You're perfectly safe," Darth said. "Nothing can go wrong as long as we don't touch anything."

I looked at him anxiously, wondering if he was telling the truth. If so, it meant he'd ruled out the possibility of a time bomb. And if he had, I wanted to know what made him *sure* there couldn't be something set to blast at any minute. I had a horrible suspicion that since the invention of digital clocks time bombs didn't have to tick.

This didn't seem an ideal time to get into the theory of bomb detection, though, so I settled for reminding myself he was an expert.

"Just have a good look at each room," he said. "Don't touch a thing. And the second you notice anything that doesn't seem normal, tell me."

I nodded, then forced one foot in front of the other along the short hallway and into the living room. I slowly swept it with my eyes. Everything looked exactly as I'd left it. Every nook and cranny.

The same was true in the kitchen and bedroom. Which only left the bathroom.

Darth Vader still on my heels, I started toward it, my heart in my throat.

The door was ajar. I cautiously stepped through the doorway...and froze.

"The shower curtain," I whispered. "I never leave the shower curtain pulled across the tub like that."

"Get out of here," Darth said, stepping back against the wall, opening a path for my escape. "Go back out into the hall."

Chapter Twelve

The moment I walked back out into the hall, Rev hugged me so tightly it felt as if he'd never let go.

I was so terrified I couldn't imagine ever wanting him to. But Frank Barboni and Darth Vader's partner were hovering on either side of us, obviously desperate to know what was going on inside my apartment. So, reluctantly, I disentangled myself from Rev's arms and told them what little there was to tell.

The number of police officers had multiplied while I'd been gone. When I asked about that, Barboni explained that my apartment would be searched with the proverbial fine-tooth comb before I could go into it again. Regardless of what had or hadn't been hidden behind the shower curtain.

Several minutes had passed since I'd left Darth Vader in the bathroom, so if there *had* been something there, at least it hadn't exploded in his face.

A moment later, he appeared in the doorway. A collective sigh of relief greeted him.

His visor was flipped up, revealing an uncertain expression. He'd removed his clumsy mitts and was holding my largest casserole dish gingerly in front of him.

His partner peered in through the glass cover and swore quietly. "That's what was in the bathtub?"

Darth nodded.

I glanced uneasily at Rev, then back at Darth.

"What is it?" Rev asked, draping his arm securely over my shoulders.

"Have a look," Darth said. He moved a couple of steps closer to us.

I took a deep breath, then looked.

At the exact instant I realized what I was seeing, Rev muttered, "Good God . . . a scorpion."

Even though the thing was trapped, my heart began beating almost as fast as it had when I'd spotted the drawn shower curtain.

The shape of a miniature black lobster, the animal was maybe four inches long, with a tail at least the length of its body. And at the end of that tail, I recalled from some long-ago biology class, was the stinger.

I couldn't remember for certain whether a scorpion's sting is fatal, but I had a horrible feeling it could be.

"I don't suppose," Barboni said, "that cobra and canary story you were talking about last night had a scorpion in it, too?"

"No," Rev told him, "but there are all kinds of scorpions in Egypt. And in its mythology. Someone's obviously intent on sending a message."

Barboni nodded in agreement, but I hadn't needed that to tell me Rev was right. Somebody was warning us, once again, to back off the mummy case claim. And my inclination to do exactly that was growing stronger and stronger.

Not that I wanted to be a quitter. But I didn't want to be dead, either.

"We're just in the way here now," Barboni said to Lisa Rashkin. "They'll be searching the apartment most of the evening," he added, turning to Rev and me. "Why don't the four of us go somewhere and see what sense we can make of this?"

"My dress," I said, suddenly remembering the reason we'd come by. "The funeral."

Barboni and Rashkin looked at me as if I was losing my marbles, so I quickly explained.

"They won't let you in there again," Barboni said. "Not until they've finished dusting and checking for evidence."

"Do you have more than one black dress?" Lisa Rashkin asked.

When I shook my head, she said, "Okay, I'll see if I can persuade someone inside to get it for you."

I gave her a grateful smile, then turned my attention back to Rev and Barboni.

"What about Mrs. Richey?" Rev was asking. "Did your fellows get anything useful from her?"

"Not much more than she told you. A little more description, but basically just that the woman looked a lot like Marina and claimed to be her sister Janet."

"Janet Koslovsky," I murmured.

"No, not Janet Koslovsky," Barboni said. "I couldn't tell you when you called on the car phone," he added quietly. "Those things are really just radios. Anyone can listen in, and we're not releasing this information yet. But Forensic ID'd the mummy earlier today. *It* was Janet Koslovsky."

THE SOMEWHERE REV AND I ended up talking with Frank Barboni and Lisa Rashkin was Rev's apartment.

He'd ordered pizza for the second night running, and we'd sat until darkness had fallen, comparing notes on what people at the Donner had told *us* with what the same people had told the police.

There was the odd discrepancy, but nothing that seemed significant. The only thing we all felt certain about was that Ashton Crawly had masterminded the theft of the mummy case. Then, presumably because she'd discovered what he'd done, he'd murdered Janet Koslovsky.

So far, though, the only evidence against Creepy Crawly was either circumstantial or hearsay. Not enough to lay charges.

And even if the police came up with something solid on Crawly, Barboni wanted to hold off tipping his hand until he'd established who *else* had been involved.

"Ashton Crawly," he'd explained, "doesn't have the talent to have made the forgery. And as far as we've been able to find out, he doesn't know a thing about explosives. So neither the bomb that killed Charlie Obregon, nor the one planted in your car, Marina, were his work. At the very least, he had one accomplice. My guess is there were *more* than one."

I swallowed hard as those words replayed in my mind, wondering just how many accomplices we were talking about. The thought of Crawly wandering around loose was bad enough. The idea of an entire gang of killers out there was even more unsettling.

But at least Barboni was sure things would move swiftly now that the body had been identified.

For starters, he intended to have another talk with Janet Koslovsky's boyfriend, Joe Callivetti. He had high hopes that Joe knew things about Janet's relationship with her boss that he hadn't initially thought to mention.

"So, let's get back to that PR woman who looks like Marina," Rev was saying to Barboni. "You think she was the one with the scorpion? That she's on Crawly's team?"

"Well...anything's possible. But Susan Dafoe couldn't have turned out that reproduction any more than Crawly could have."

"Her resemblance to Marina," Lisa Rashkin put in, "is the only suspicious thing about her at the moment. But if she *was* the woman Mrs. Richey let in, she had to be away from the Donner for part of the afternoon. We can check that out first thing tomorrow."

"So I guess that's about it for now," Barboni said, nodding to Lisa that they should get going.

Rev and I trailed after them to the door.

Barboni paused, his hand on the knob. "Look," he said to me, "I know you've got a job to do. But I don't want you anywhere near the Donner for the next few days. Either of you," he added, glancing at Rev. "Understood?"

I nodded. Maybe I was a dreadful chicken, but I felt more than a little relieved at being officially told to back off for a while.

He opened the door, then hesitated once more, saying, "Guess we'll be seeing you tomorrow afternoon. Funny thing about murderers. Sometimes they just can't resist showing up at the victim's funeral, so we always like to keep an eye out, see exactly who's there."

A weak goodbye smile was the best I could manage. I'd be lucky if thinking about the funeral didn't give me nightmares tonight. And tomorrow...well, I wasn't looking forward to tomorrow at all.

Barboni and Rashkin wouldn't be the only ones keeping an eye out at the funeral. Because logic said that whoever had planted the bomb in Charlie's car had to be the same person who'd planted the one in mine.

AFTER THE DETECTIVES LEFT, I changed into my jeans and a sweatshirt. Then I phoned Nat Fishbein, as promised, to fill him in on what had been happening since we'd talked last night.

"Holy shmoley," he muttered when I was done. "Enough's gone on to fill twenty-four days, never mind twenty-four hours."

"Well . . . time flies when you're having fun, right?"

Nat laughed at that, but I knew he was only being polite because he cut the laugh off abruptly and said, "Are you staying at this Revington guy's apartment again tonight?"

"I . . . I guess so." I glanced down at the sofa bed I was sitting on and absently smoothed my hand across the bright patchwork quilt. Neither Rev nor I had bothered folding the bed back into a sofa this morning. And I hadn't, I realized, had even a single thought about going home tonight.

"That's a good idea," Nat was saying. "And be sure and do what that cop told you. Keep away from the Donner."

"I will."

"And be careful."

"Nat, you told me that yesterday. I haven't forgotten."

"So what? It won't hurt you to hear it again. Hell, I'd give anything to be out of this damned hospital and back on the job with you. But they're not letting me out yet. Told me I can't even go to Charlie's funeral."

I closed my eyes, wishing someone had told *me* I couldn't go. My emotional reservoir was already drained.

Nat and I said our goodbyes, then I simply sat on the bed, lost in thought.

After a few minutes, Rev appeared in the doorway. He'd changed into jeans, as well, topped off by a cotton sweater the same slate blue as his eyes.

He stood watching me. One shoulder rested against the side of the doorway, making his sweater pull taut across his chest, emphasizing its breadth. His jeans stretched provocatively across his hips.

Merely looking at him made me think of last night, about how safe and warm I'd felt in his arms.

"What are you thinking?" he asked.

"The truth?"

"Yeah, the truth."

I hesitated, knowing where the truth might lead and not sure I was ready for that. But if ever I'd wanted a little warmth and reassurance, now was the time.

"I was thinking I need a hug," I said quietly. "You know? Like when you were seven years old and something awful happened? And you felt as if the whole world was out to get you? But all your mother or father had to do was hug you and things seemed better?"

"Yeah...I know." He crossed to the sofa bed and sat down beside me, putting his arms around me and drawing me close.

His raw, earthy, masculine scent enveloped me. It was distinctly Revington York, and more seductively tantalizing than any men's cologne I'd ever smelled.

My arms around his waist, I rested my cheek on his chest.

"It isn't surprising you feel shaky, you know," he said, stroking my hair. "Things have been moving too fast to cope with. It's as if we got tossed into a time accelerator the day we met."

I shifted a little in his arms, so that I could see his face. "You're right. That's *exactly* what it's like. So much has happened in the past few days...it seems like a million years since I first walked into your office."

"Yeah...so much has happened," he murmured, trailing his fingers softly down my neck.

I reminded myself that it *had* been only a few days since Rev and I had met. I still knew almost nothing about him. And he seemed intent on keeping his past a deep, dark secret.

But his merest touch turned me to jelly.

"You know, Marina...one of the things that's happened since you first walked into my office..."

"Is what?" I whispered, even though I didn't really need to ask. I'd never seen a clearer message in anyone's eyes.

Incredible as it seemed, impossibly fast as I knew it was, I suddenly felt positive that Rev had been falling in love with me, just as I'd been falling in love with him.

I hadn't wanted to admit what was happening. Not even to myself.

But now that I had, I felt like laughing and crying at the same time. How could two people possibly fall in love under such crazy circumstances?

I gave Rev another tentative smile and brushed my fingers across the eight-o'clock shadow on his chin.

It was enough to make him pull me closer once more, igniting a fire deep within me.

"Marina, look," he murmured. "I didn't expect to find myself feeling anything for you. And I sure didn't expect you'd feel anything for me . . . but you do, don't you?''

Afraid to say anything, I simply nodded. I was far better off listening than talking.

If I opened my mouth, I'd end up telling him I felt more for him than I ever had for any other man. So much more that it had gone way beyond a measurable amount.

"Marina . . . oh, hell, I can't explain this. Not here and now. Maybe later . . . maybe sometime . . ."

Those weren't the words I wanted to hear. They weren't even close. "Rev?" I managed to say, drawing back a little again and gazing at him.

He took his arms from around me and shook his head, saying, "I can't do this, Marina. Something casual I could handle. But I can't let myself get beyond casual. Not with *any* woman. I . . . look, I'm sorry. This isn't the time or place. It's just that every minute I'm with you . . . it's like I've known all along I had to put on the brakes but I didn't want to. But . . . let's just drop it, all right?"

All right? After that incomprehensible little speech? After the look in his eyes? If the man thought I'd actually let this drop, he was was out of his mind.

"Rev . . . maybe this *isn't* the ideal time or place for whatever you're talking about. But now that you've started, you can hardly leave me hanging. Exactly what were you trying to say?"

"Dammit, Marina, I wish I could explain it better, but I can't even do that."

"Try," I demanded, doing my utmost to ignore the way my eyes and throat were burning. "Have you got a wife you love hidden away somewhere? Is that it?"

The Research file had said he was single. But Research was no more perfect than any other department at Sherwin McNee.

"No, I'm not married, Marina. I never have been."

I took a deep, calming breath. "And you're not on the run from the law?"

He hesitated for a split second—or maybe I only imagined that—then said, "No."

"You have a terminal illness," I tried, praying that wasn't it, either.

"No. Marina, leave it. Please? It's not something I can talk about."

"Not even with me?" I could feel tears of frustration forming. If he hadn't *wanted* to put on the brakes, didn't I at least deserve to know why he was doing it, anyway?

"I *especially* can't talk about it with you," he said.

Even though I tried desperately to blink them back, the tears began escaping.

"Oh, Marina," he whispered, brushing them away. "Hey, don't cry."

I stared down at the patchwork quilt on the sofa bed, suppressing a sob. The patches were infuriatingly fuzzy around the edges, and I concentrated on tracing the outline of a large red one, as if delineating its border was crucial to my well-being.

"Dammit," Rev muttered so quietly I knew he was talking to himself, not to me. "Dammit, the last thing in the world I meant to do was fall in love with you."

My vision still blurred, I looked up.

Slowly, he shook his head. "And the second last thing in the world I meant to do was let you *realize* I'd fallen in love with you."

"Rev..." I swallowed fresh tears. He'd said he'd fallen in love with me. How could I cry after hearing that? "Rev...I don't believe there's anything so awful in your past that you can't tell me."

"It isn't so awful...it's just...it's just that I can't talk about it."

It wasn't so awful. That wasn't much, but it was a start. And it was going to have to be enough for the moment. I knew pushing any harder now would be a mistake.

A few minutes ago he'd said, "Maybe later...maybe sometime..." So I'd just have to wait.

"All right," I whispered. "All right, I won't ask anything more. But can I tell you something?"

"What?"

"I...Rev, you're not the only one who managed to fall in love without meaning to. It must be one of the side effects of being tossed into a time accelerator."

He gave me the slowest, sexiest smile I'd ever seen. It did a lot to make me feel less upset. And the less upset I felt, the more aware I grew of the utterly scrumptious, hotter-than-hot sensations that were beginning to race through my body.

After a few moments, Rev draped his arms around my neck and fiddled with the clasp on the mummy beads until it came undone. He put them on the bedside table and switched off the lamp.

Only the palest of moon shadows strayed in through the window, barely enough light to let me still make out the chiseled angles of his face.

I ran my fingers along his jaw, and he smoothed his hands up my back, resting them on my neck, drawing me closer for a kiss.

It was all I could do to brush my fingers across his lips, telling him to wait. But I had to explain. "Rev...what you said about *casual*...about not being able to have anything *more* than that...I'm not into casual."

"I knew you wouldn't be," he whispered. "That's why I knew I had to put on the brakes."

"But you didn't."

"No...I couldn't."

His mouth was so close to mine the warmth of his breath fanned my lips, intensifying those hotter-than-hot sensations until they became a full-blown wildfire that threatened to consume me.

I leaned into his kiss with my entire body, caressing his back, his neck, then tangling my fingers in his hair as he pressed me down onto the quilt.

I craved this man. There was no other way of putting it. I needed his kisses and his touch as much as I needed to breathe, and the realization both thrilled and terrified me. I loved Revington York but I didn't know him. Not nearly as completely as I wanted to. There was that mysterious something in his past he wouldn't talk about.

But this was the present, not the past. And all that seemed important in the present was how very much I loved him...and that he was making me certain I'd die if I couldn't have him.

We undressed while we kissed, as if even a few seconds without his lips on mine would be an eternity.

And then he ran his fingers lightly down my naked body, murmuring, "Oh, Lord, Marina," before he began kissing me again.

Hot with longing, slick with desire, I was melting inside, as hungry for Rev as he clearly was for me.

His kisses grew deeper and more demanding. His body heat, his hardness, his elemental maleness, all combined to heighten my responses.

As I grew impossibly aroused, his caresses became ever more intimate, more possessive, until I couldn't stand the delicious torture of his touch for a moment longer.

Urgently, almost incoherently, I murmured his name. And that was the last word either of us spoke until the force of our passion had subsided and we lay tangled in each other's arms.

Making love with Revington York was like nothing I'd ever experienced. It was consuming and overwhelming and fulfilling and utterly heavenly.

I felt complete. Even though I'd never before realized that anything was missing. I never wanted to move from the warm shelter of Rev's embrace. This was where I belonged, his arms around me, his hand resting comfortably on my breast.

"You asleep?" he whispered at last.

"Yes."

He nuzzled my neck. "Then there's no point in telling you I love you, is there?"

"Mmmm . . . that might be worth waking up for." I smiled at him in the darkness. "How much?"

"How much what?"

"How much do you love me?"

"More than I can say."

"More than your Porsche?" I teased.

"More than a whole fleet of them."

I kissed his chest, tempted to ask again about the deep, dark secret of his past. But I resisted. He loved me. That meant he'd tell me sooner or later.

In the meantime, I snuggled even closer to him and slept deeply until morning light woke me.

Morning light and the faint aroma of fresh coffee.

For a second my mind refused to focus. Then recollections of last night came flooding back, and I could feel myself smiling a smile that would make the Cheshire cat look like a grump.

I snuggled under the patchwork quilt, willing Rev to come back to bed.

A few long minutes later he appeared, wearing a robe and carrying a tray with two steaming mugs on it. His eyes had a tinge of uncertainty in them—but only for a moment.

Apparently, I looked every bit as happy as I felt because he grinned at me, saying, "How would you feel about this coffee getting a little cold before we drink it?"

"Cold coffee's my absolutely favorite thing in the world."

"Your absolute favorite thing?" he said, setting a world's record for putting down a tray, throwing off a robe and crawling into a sofa bed.

"Well...*one* of my absolute favorite things." I didn't have a chance to enumerate the others because Rev's lips got in the way.

Chapter Thirteen

After an hour of morning lovemaking with Rev the day had nowhere to go but downhill, and our coffee having grown cold was the least of it.

Since Frank Barboni had ordered us to stay away from the Donner, I decided I'd better make an appearance at Sherwin McNee. Rev dropped me off, then continued on his way to Careful Wheels, promising to meet me at O'Conner's Funeral Home a little before two.

He'd suggested lunch, but I'd doubted I'd be up to that. And I'd been right. The atmosphere in Special Claims made me feel as if Charlie's wake was already in progress. By the time I got to O'Conner's I was fighting back tears.

I made it numbly through both the service and the interment, clutching Rev's hand like a lifeline.

As promised, Frank Barboni and Lisa Rashkin were at the funeral, but if they saw anybody they thought looked suspicious among the mourners they didn't let on to Rev or me.

They did tell us two things, though. The first was that the police had finished with my Mustang. It was back in my parking space at my apartment, and the keys were in my mailbox. The second thing was that Susan Dafoe, the Donner's PR lady, hadn't been away from the museum for even a minute yesterday afternoon. So we were at square one again with the question of who had posed as my sister and delivered the scorpion.

After the graveside service was over, Rev and I headed back to his apartment, changed into jeans and brooded.

At least *I* brooded. He force-fed me chicken soup for dinner, then made several attempts to cheer me up. Cheerful wasn't on my evening's agenda, though. When I wasn't thinking about the funeral, I was worrying if I'd *ever* again feel safe in my own apartment.

Finally, Rev threw in the towel and simply sat with his arm around my shoulders and his nose buried in a book.

While he read, I mentally sifted through everything I'd learned about the mummy case, hoping a brilliant flash of insight would miraculously strike. But brilliant flashes of insight didn't turn out to be on the evening's agenda, either.

"I feel so frustrated," I said at last. "Aside from Crawly, we don't have any more sense of who's involved in all this than we did at the start. There must be something we could be doing to try to figure things out, instead of sitting here like bumps on a log."

"It's past nine," he pointed out. "Exactly what do you think we could be doing?"

"I don't know. But *something*. There has to be a clue we've all missed. You, me, the police, all of us. Some detail about the way the work of mounting the exhibit had been organized that would tell us who was working with Crawly."

Rev closed his book and put it onto the coffee table, saying, "You want to go to Careful Wheels? Check through all the paperwork I've got on file? See if anything leaps out at you?"

"Have the police looked through it yet?"

"No. When the switch was discovered, they said they'd want to. But nobody's shown up yet."

"Let's give it a shot, then." I knew the odds of turning up anything were so low it probably wasn't worth the effort, but at least it was better than doing nothing.

CAREFUL WHEELS' RECORDS on transporting the Egyptian exhibit were far more extensive than I'd expected.

When we stacked everything on Rachel's desk, the pile was so high that the top folders slid off, knocking Rev's keys to the floor.

He picked them up and threw them onto the filing cabinet, then began sorting through the material.

There was correspondence with both the Donner and the L.A. museum, the contract to transport the items, the drivers' log for their trip, and several large, fat, sealed envelopes.

"Wonder what's in these?" he said, turning one of them over in his hand. There was nothing written on either side.

He slit the end of the envelope with his thumb and dumped the contents. Color photographs spilled out onto the desk. At least thirty, all eight-by-ten glossies of various exhibit pieces.

"That's strange," he said. "I didn't ask anyone for pictures. Shows how often I look in here. Rachel takes care of all the filing."

He grabbed another of the envelopes. By the time he'd ripped them all open, there was a huge stack of photos, along with a copy of a letter that explained how they'd come to be in the file.

Only a few days after the Donner people had signed Careful Wheels' contract, Rachel had written to the L.A. museum, requesting color pictures of each item that was going to be shipped.

"What possible use did she figure these would be?" Rev muttered, staring at the prints.

"You're sure you didn't ask her to get them?"

"No...but she has a lot of initiative. She's done things like that before. Taken something on, herself, without bothering to ask me about it."

Since Rachel brought out my catty side, I bit my tongue. But I couldn't help thinking she'd taken it on herself to ask an awful lot of the museum, for no apparent reason.

No *apparent* reason, I silently repeated.

"Maybe it's worth a closer look at these," I said aloud, starting to gather them up. "Why don't I take them into your office and go through them while you read over the correspondence?"

Rev didn't look as if he thought much of the suggestion, but he merely shrugged, so I carted them away. Only half a dozen or so slid off the stack before I made it to his desk.

I retraced my steps, collecting the strays, then sat down in Rev's leather chair and began going through the pile.

"Marina?" he called when I was about half done. "There's a little gray phone book at the front of my top drawer. Will you give me Scott Usher's home number from it? There's something in one of these letters I'm not clear on. Maybe he'll know what it means."

I found the number, called it to Rev, and was putting the book away when I noticed the corner of a snapshot sticking out of a manila folder at the back of the drawer.

From the outer office, I could hear Rev starting to dial. It took about half a second for my curiosity to win out over my reluctance to peek, and I reached for the folder.

When I pulled it out I got a surprise. It had been concealing a pistol. A black semiautomatic, similar to the one Nat Fishbein carries. Seeing it started me wondering, once more, what secrets Rev was keeping.

I dragged my eyes from the gun and flipped open the folder. The snapshot inside was of four people standing on a pier, in front of a large sailboat that bore the name *Katie's Pride*.

There were a couple in their late fifties, Rev, and a woman who was about his age. Maybe a little younger. He had his arm around her, and she was gazing at him as if she positively adored him.

A queasy feeling hit me. I told myself it was the picture of the boat. Practically anything can make me feel seasick. But I knew it was the woman, not the boat, that had caused my problem.

She was gorgeous. A strawberry-blonde with big blue eyes. And while Rev had said he'd never been married, he hadn't said he'd never been in love.

What did you expect? I asked myself. He's thirty-two years old. And he's never said a word about spending thirty-two years in a monastery. Besides, whatever the woman might have been to him, she wasn't with him now. That's what was important.

Despite my self-directed lecture, the queasy feeling remained. And I couldn't stop wondering if the strawberry-blonde was named Katie.

I turned my attention to the older couple. Rev had told me he had no family. But he must have had parents until some point. Was that who these people were?

I had no more way of knowing that than of knowing anything about the strawberry-blonde. The snapshot might have been a few years old or might have been taken a month ago. Rev didn't look any different in it than he did now.

Carefully, I put the picture back inside the folder and slipped it in on top of the gun again, wishing I'd never taken it out.

My intuition was saying that the reason Rev wouldn't talk about his past had something to do with those people. But I had no idea what that reason was. And I knew I didn't have the nerve to ask him about them.

"Not home," he called from the other room.

"Pardon?"

"No answer at Scott's."

"Oh...too bad."

I sat staring at the pile of photos on the desk again, trying to force my mind back to them. It was difficult. My thoughts kept returning to the snapshot...and the gun.

It was probably my wandering concentration that kept me from realizing what wasn't right about the pictures. I merely had a sense that *something* wasn't.

I was halfway through the pile for the second time before it finally struck me what was wrong.

"Rev?" I called, my voice sounding a little shaky to me.

It must have sounded more than a *little* shaky to him, because he came racing into his office, looking as if he expected to find both a cobra and a scorpion in there with me.

"The photographs," I said. "Rev, there are three or four different shots of all the exhibit pieces. Except for the mummy case. There isn't a single, solitary one of it."

Rev stared at the stack of prints for a moment, then looked at me again.

"I'm positive," I said before he asked. "Not a single, solitary one."

"But that was the prize piece of the exhibit. Why wouldn't they have sent shots of it?"

"I'm sure they would have. Rachel's letter asked for photos of *each* piece that was going to be shipped. Rev...have you thought of *any* logical reason she might have asked for all these pictures?"

He shook his head.

"Then do you think it's possible..." I paused, not certain if I was off on a wild goose chase or if what I was wondering actually made sense.

"Do I think what's possible?" Rev demanded.

"Do you think maybe all Rachel *really* wanted was pictures of the mummy case? That she only asked for pictures of *everything* as a cover?"

"Wanted pictures of the mummy case," Rev said in slow, measured words. "So that someone could use them to make a reproduction?"

I nodded.

Rev swore, shaking his head. "Rachel?" he muttered. "Rachel had something to do with all this?"

"Does anything else add up?"

"I don't know...nothing comes to mind. But Rachel working with Ashton Crawly?"

"Does she know him?"

"Hell, I have no idea. She could. We've done previous work for the Donner. Or Scott might have introduced them some time or other. But..." Rev stopped mid-sentence and began rubbing his jaw thoughtfully.

"But what?" I pressed.

"But Crawly already had pictures of the exhibit pieces. Remember Mavis Hoskins telling us how they chose the items to copy for the gift shop? She said Crawly had pictures from the L.A. museum and they used them to decide."

For half a second, I started to erase my suspicions, then I shook my head. "Creepy Crawly only had pictures of things for them to choose from. *That's* what Mavis Hoskins told us. And those would just have been pictures of the small items. They'd never have even considered making reproductions of the mummy case."

"You're right," Rev said. "So when Crawly needed help with that angle he used Rachel as his little helper. Dammit. To think my own secretary would stab me in the back."

"Don't say that," I murmured. "We've already had Janet Koslovsky suffocated and Charlie Obregon blown to bits. The last thing we need is you stabbed to death."

WE SEARCHED every square inch of Rachel's desk. Every square inch, that is, except for the locked bottom drawer.

But even it didn't slow us down for long. Rev got a hammer from the storage section of the building and simply smashed the lock.

If we'd added things up wrong, if it turned out that Rachel *hadn't* actually been working for Crawly, Rev was going to be awfully embarrassed when he had to tell her what had happened to her desk.

But it quickly became clear that we hadn't added things up wrong.

In the back of the drawer we discovered what I thought, for a horrified second, was a dead animal.

It wasn't. But it was horrifying all the same. A wig of long, straight brown hair. The same color as mine.

Staring at it couldn't have made me feel creepier if it *had* been a dead animal.

"It never even occurred to me," Rev muttered. "But Rachel's about your size. And with that on, it's no wonder Mrs. Richey believed she was your sister."

"Which explains who got into my apartment with the scorpion," I said. "But we still don't know who got into your place with the snake. Or even *how* they got in."

Rev glanced at the top of the filing cabinet, saying, "I have a bad habit of leaving my keys lying around the office. Rachel is always having to find them for me. And there's a place just down the street that cuts copies."

"I think it's safe to conclude," I said uneasily, "that Rachel had more to do with things than just getting Ashton Crawly the pictures."

"Yeah, I'd say she was one busy lady. Buying wigs, toting around snakes and scorpions. And who the hell knows what else she was up to?"

"So...our next move should be calling Barboni, shouldn't it?"

Rev nodded. "Let's just finish what we're doing first. See if we can find anything else."

We pulled the bottom drawer all the way out, and I checked for something taped underneath or behind it. There was nothing.

"The garbage is next." I sat down on the floor, glad I was wearing jeans. "You never know what you'll find."

Unceremoniously, I dumped the trash basket.

Several pop cans clattered onto the floor, along with about twenty wadded-up balls of paper.

Rachel, I thought, eyeing the cans, wasn't into recycling. But that was undoubtedly the least of her sins.

Rev dropped to the floor beside me and began unwadding one of the balls.

It was immediately apparent that Rachel was a doodler. Most of the sheets of paper bore sketches or circles or words written at weird angles on them.

"Marina?" Rev said.

When I glanced over he was gazing at one of the smoothed-out pages. "Look at this." He handed it to me. "Look what she's written in the corner, there."

I sat gazing at the cryptic note. Scrawled across the corner, circled about a hundred times, was "11 museum." My heart pounding harder than normal, I glanced at Rev again. "Does this garbage get emptied every day?"

"First thing in the morning. The cleaner's been and gone before Rachel or I get here."

"So this was thrown out today." I checked my watch. "It's after ten-thirty."

Rev shoved himself up off the floor. "You think that means eleven tonight? And the museum is the Donner?" he asked, giving me a hand up.

"I think it's worth a shot."

Before we left, Rev got the gun from his desk and tucked it into the waistband of his jeans, snug against the small of his back.

He made no effort to hide what he was doing, and I didn't ask if he had a permit to carry a gun. Partly because, permit or no permit, I wanted him to take the gun along.

I wasn't much of a shot yet. And I'd never fired my snubby at anything except a target. But Crawly was a killer. And somebody else, somebody who knew how to plant car bombs, was a killer, too.

So instead of saying another word about Rev's gun, I said, "We'd better call Barboni before we leave. Let him know what we're doing."

"We'll use the car phone," Rev said. "We don't have any time to waste."

With the Porsche racing along Market, Rev started to call Barboni. He had almost the entire phone number punched in before I realized we were making a mistake.

"Rev, wait," I said.

He stopped mid-punch, glancing a question at me.

"Remember what Barboni told us? That anyone can listen in to car phones? And if Rachel was smart enough to copy your keys and get hold of a snake and a scorpion, she's smart enough to think about listening in on your calls."

"Dammit," he muttered. "What do you want to do, then? Find a pay phone?"

"It's already past eleven," I said, glancing at my watch. "And Barboni was on duty all day, so he won't be on tonight. Which means we'd have to wait at the phone until he called back. I think..."

I hesitated. I was scared to death, but I wasn't going to stop being scared until this was over. And the longer it took until it was over, the more chance there was that somebody else would end up dead.

The most likely *somebodies* being Rev and me.

"Let's just check things out ourselves first," I finally said, trying to ignore the rush of anxiety I felt at my own words. "See if there's a sign of anyone around the Donner. Maybe what Rachel wrote down meant something else entirely."

"Sure," Rev said, flashing me an anxious grin. "Just like there was actually a teacup in that gift box."

REV SWITCHED OFF his headlights as we neared the Donner, but with the bright streetlights, the difference was barely perceptible.

I stared through the windshield at the museum, trying to forget that Barboni had ordered us to stay away from it. And that Nat Fishbein had told me the same thing. And that two people were already dead.

In the darkness, the building looked like a gray fortress. It cast a pale, eerie glow out into the night, with just enough lights on inside for the guards to make their rounds.

Outside, there was no sign of activity.

We drove on by, and Rev turned down an alley that ran along the museum's west side.

The second we left Ocean Avenue, darkness surrounded us. But the moon was almost full, and my eyes quickly began adjusting.

I gazed ahead, watching for the entrance to the shipping and receiving area. The gate would be closed and locked...unless something was going on that shouldn't be.

All at once, the entrance loomed ahead on our left.

My breath caught in my throat.

The gate was standing ajar.

"They'll hear us," I whispered. The Porsche's throaty growl suddenly seemed so loud I was certain anyone within two blocks would know we were coming.

Rev cut the ignition and let the car glide to a silent stop.

When we'd left Careful Wheels, he'd put his gun into the glove compartment. While he retrieved it, I took my snubby out of my bag.

"Leave your purse in the car," Rev said. "You may need both hands."

I stashed the bag onto the floor, deciding not to ask what he thought I might need both hands for. Hands that were shaking.

We got out of the Porsche and quietly closed the doors.

Rev stuck his gun in the waistband of his jeans again, so I followed his example, wishing with all my might I was wearing a jacket with a pocket instead of a sweatshirt without one.

The idea of the business end of a gun pointing at the base of my spinal cord terrified me. If the thing went off, I'd be either dead or paralyzed.

Rev took my hand and we started toward the open gate, hugging the wall of the museum, with me reminding myself guns almost never discharge accidentally. According to my shooting instructor, at least.

We reached the gate and paused, gazing across the concrete expanse between us and the loading dock.

Two vehicles were parked beside it. A sported-up white Ford Escort and a burgundy Magic Wagon with its side door wide open. The two rear seats, I noted, had been removed.

"That's Rachel's car," Rev murmured.

"And the van?"

He shook his head, saying he didn't recognize it.

Gazing at it, I absently fingered the mummy beads. I was hoping that touching them would calm me, but it did a whole lot more.

Abruptly, amazingly, the pieces of the puzzle all fell neatly into place. I was almost too startled to be frightened.

In my mind's eye, I could literally see what had happened. A series of action scenes unfolded as if I were watching a movie.

Everything was crystal clear. Everything except the identities of the actors. They were only foggy silhouettes. There were three of them, but not even their genders were discernible.

"That's how they did it," I whispered. I hadn't made a conscious effort to speak. The words just slipped out.

"The real mummy case is still in the museum," I murmured, answering Rev's silent question. "After it was delivered, the forgery was substituted. It . . ."

I closed my eyes and could visualize one of the shadowy figures working with artist's tools. "Someone made the forgery right in the Donner. In one of the workshops . . . it's all dusty and crowded with crates . . . must have been a workshop that was hardly ever used."

I opened my eyes again. My hand was still resting on the beads and Rev was staring at them.

When I caught his gaze he cleared his throat uneasily, then said, "I guess that could be what happened, all right, but—"

"It *is* what happened. I... I just saw images. In my mind."

"Images."

"Yes. Of how they did it. They made the switch after hours, between the guards' rounds. And they hid the real case away until they had a chance to get it out of the building."

"They?" Rev said. "This *they* is Crawly and Rachel?"

"That part wasn't clear. There were *three* people. That's all I could tell."

Rev's gaze flickered back to my necklace, and he stood rubbing his jaw.

Self-consciously, I tucked the mummy beads out of sight, under the neckband of my sweatshirt. We both knew how I'd gotten those images. There was no point dwelling on it.

"All right," he said at last, giving me an anxious smile. "Let's say you've got everything figured right. That has to mean that they came tonight with the van to..."

"Exactly." There was plenty of space to put even a crated mummy case into that Magic Wagon.

"And they're in there now," Rev said. "Must have bridged the security system, somehow. And the mummy case is on its way out."

"We can't let that happen," I murmured, fingering my beads again. If they loaded the case and Princess Amonit's mummy into the van and got away...

I was more upset, I suddenly realized, at the thought of them getting away with the mummy herself than with the priceless mummy case. Mr. Leibranch and Nat Fishbein would have fits if they knew that.

"The van is probably Crawly's," Rev said.

I nodded. Creepy Crawly was inside the museum with Rachel. And maybe a third person.

However many we were talking about, though, they were . . . well, I didn't know exactly what they were doing at this precise moment, but the way Rev was dragging me along toward the building again, we'd be finding out any minute.

Chapter Fourteen

Rev and I crept across the remaining few yards of darkness like a couple of cat burglars.

Only minutes ago, I'd been glad there was a full moon to help me see. Now I was wishing the night were pitch black. If anyone spotted us...and if the anyone had a gun...

Directly ahead, its surface about eye level, stood the loading dock. About fifteen feet along it, to the left, was a receiving door so large you could have backed a truck through it. Straight ahead was a smaller door, just somewhat oversized. Both were closed, but I knew from our visit to the Shipping department that both led into it.

We reached the dock, and Rev pulled me down beneath the shelter of its overhang.

"We need a plan," he whispered.

I'd been so caught up in the moment I hadn't been thinking. But what on earth were we doing? We were ordinary people, not commandos.

"Okay, this is how we play it," he said quietly, handing me his keys. "You wait here. If Rachel *is* tuned into the car phone frequency, we sure don't want to tip our hand. But if you hear any commotion inside, run like hell back to the car and call nine-one-one."

"What?"

"I said—"

"I heard what you said! But if you think you're going inside, when we know there are at least two of *them* in there, you're—"

"Of course I'm going in. What the hell did you think I was going to do?"

"I don't know. Have a look, I guess. See what we could see. But now we've seen as much as we need to, so—"

"Dammit, Marina, don't—"

"Don't you "dammit, Marina" me! We're not part of a SWAT team. We'll *both* go back to the car and call the police. Right now. And if Rachel's listening in . . . well, we'll worry about that if it happens."

Rev was opening his mouth to retort when we heard the tiny creaking noise of a door opening almost directly above us. He swallowed his words as a shaft of pale yellow light spilled down onto the parking area.

Heart hammering, I pressed myself flat against the dock.

"All clear," a woman's voice whispered into the night. "But we'll have to get it out fast. That guard's due by again in ten minutes."

There was a second creaking noise, and the shaft of light vanished. A quiet click told us the door had shut again.

I waited, not breathing, until I felt sure the woman had really gone back inside and wasn't standing on the dock above us. Then I whispered, "That was Rachel?"

Rev nodded. "And you heard her. It had to be the mummy case she was talking about getting out. So we've got no choice. The cops might not make it here fast enough. I'll go in and you stay out here as backup."

"No way! I'm going with you."

Either I'd sounded a million times braver than I felt or Rev had realized how stubborn I can be, because he simply swung himself onto the dock, then gave me a hand up.

"For God's sake be careful," he whispered, drawing his gun and starting across the platform.

I crept along behind him, pulling the snubby out of my waistband as we reached the door and trying to convince myself I wasn't completely and utterly terrified.

I couldn't fool myself on that one, but I wasn't going to let Rev walk in there alone and get his head blown off because there was nobody to cover his backside.

A little click, another tiny creak, and he had the door open. We slipped inside, noiselessly closing the door.

The only illumination came from a row of pale fluorescents near the center of the shipping area. The light cast eerie shadows over the shapes of crates and equipment.

On the far wall another door stood open, leading into an almost-dark hallway. Rev and I headed across the concrete floor and out into the hall, our sneakers making tiny squeaking sounds. There wasn't a security guard in sight, but I expected one to materialize any second. And I was certain it would be one with his gun cocked.

Without a moment's hesitation, Rev started off to our right. I followed along, wanting to ask if he actually knew where we were going, but afraid even to whisper.

When we reached the junction of two corridors, we paused. To the left, things were dark and silent. Twenty feet down the right hallway, though, the door of a room stood open. A rectangle of light cut through the darkness, pale enough that it might have come from a single fluorescent tube.

"Workshops," Rev whispered. "That's what those rooms are."

I nodded. When we'd had our tour of the museum, he'd obviously paid more attention to the layout than I had.

As we started toward the lit room, I began thinking about the hundreds of horrible things that might be about to happen.

We were almost at the doorway when someone inside the workshop muttered something. It was a man's voice; his words were indistinct. We tried to make ourselves invisible against the wall.

There was a scraping sound and he muttered again, more clearly this time. "If it hadn't slipped off the damned dolly we'd be home-free by now."

Rev shot me a glance that said "watch yourself," then raised his gun. Clutching the handle with both hands, he wheeled away from the wall and into the doorway, yelling, "Nobody move!"

The man swore. A woman did as well. Rachel's voice again.

"Nobody move," Rev said a second time. "Neither of you move a muscle."

I couldn't see into the room from where I was standing, but clearly he had the situation under control. Nothing horrible was happening, after all.

Still, my heart was pounding and my hands were so wet with perspiration that I was afraid my snubby would slip from my grasp. I quickly tucked it into the front of my waistband, snug against my hipbone, pulled my sweatshirt back down over it and wiped my palms on my jeans.

Rev stepped forward, pointing his gun before him.

I followed him into the dim workshop...and a sense of shock replaced much of the fear I'd been feeling. The man with Rachel wasn't Ashton Crawly. It was Scott Usher. Friendly, helpful Scott was one of the bad guys.

He and Rachel were both staring at Rev with expressions of horrified surprise on their faces.

Scott had a wooden crate levered halfway onto a dolly in front of him. A crate about six feet long by four feet wide and deep. I had no doubt it held the mummy case.

"Okay," Rev told them. "Put your hands in the air and move away from that thing."

"Rev?" Rachel said, not moving. "What's going on?"

"You tell me."

She flashed him a smile, but it wasn't her patented zillion-watt one, and it didn't look sincere. "I'm just helping Scott with something he's working on," she said.

"Something like the mummy case?"

Nervously, I glanced around as they spoke, a chill running up my spine when I realized this was the workshop I'd visualized earlier.

It was large, with room for four workbenches, but was apparently used mostly for storage. Crates and boxes stood everywhere, offering a hundred shadowy places where someone could hide.

I hadn't forgotten that my mind's eye had seen *three* foggy silhouettes. What if someone else was in here? Someone who'd been hidden from sight when Rev burst in?

I glanced at him, wondering if he remembered me saying there were three people involved in this, but I couldn't catch his eye. His attention was solely on Rachel and Scott.

"Where's Ashton Crawly?" I demanded.

"Ashton Crawly?" Rachel repeated. "How on earth would we know?"

"I don't know what you two are doing here," Scott said. "Or what the hell that gun's for. Like Rachel told you, I'm just working late and she came by to help."

"Get away from the crate," Rev snapped. "Move over by that wall."

They started to step back, then Rachel's expression changed slightly.

A warning bell went off in my head, but I wasn't fast enough. Before I could turn, someone clamped a hand over my mouth from behind and pulled me off balance.

I'D FROZEN IN PANIC. For a second or a minute. I had no idea how long my brain had been on pause, but when it clicked back into action there was still a large hand over my mouth and a large body pressed against my back.

There was also, I realized with heart-stopping terror, something that felt like a gun barrel digging into my ribs.

Rev's gun was hanging limply in his hand, and he was looking at me with desperation in his eyes.

"Man, I'm sure glad to see you," Scott was saying to whoever was holding me.

I could feel my own gun tucked against my hipbone, but there was no way I could get at it without everyone seeing. Besides which, I was too petrified to try for it.

"Okay, buddy," the man holding me said. "Put down that gun. Nice and easy."

Slowly, Rev lowered his gun to the floor.

"Shove it toward me," the man ordered. "Now, what the hell's going on here?" he demanded once Rev had slid the gun over.

"Are you in on this with these two?" Rev asked him.

"Don't even talk to this guy," Rachel snapped. "He's a lunatic. Just appeared from nowhere and—"

"You, Mr. Usher," the man interrupted. "You explain, please."

"Marina," Rev said quietly. "The man holding you is a security guard. Would you mind letting her go now?" he asked politely, gazing over my shoulder. "You're the only one with a gun."

The man didn't answer, but a moment later he took his hand from my mouth and stepped back.

My legs were trembling so badly I almost collapsed when he let go of me.

"Over by your friend, lady," he said.

I managed the few steps to Rev's side, then turned to see whose prisoner I'd been. As Rev had told me, the man was a security guard—heavy-set, in his forties.

"Okay," he said. He bent and picked up Rev's gun with his left hand, keeping his own gun pointed directly at Rev.

As he straightened up again, his glance flickered to Scott Usher. "What's the story here?"

Scott threw up his hands, managing to look completely mystified. "I stayed after closing to catch up on some work. You know that. When you made your rounds, you saw me in my office."

The man nodded.

"My girlfriend, here, came to pick me up," Scott went on, gesturing toward Rachel. "Whenever she's done that before, it's been right at five. So she's parked out back and I've gone out that way. At any rate, I forgot to tell her she'd have to buzz at the front tonight. So I went down to the receiving door and let her in."

"How'd you unlock the door without activating the alarm?" the guard said.

He sounded suspicious. I began breathing a tiny bit easier.

"Ahh...well, Mr. Griston once showed me how to switch off the alarm. He wanted me to know how because...oh, the details don't matter right now. The point is that it seemed silly to bother you guys when I could open up on my own. But before I got things locked again, these two forced their way in and dragged us down here at gunpoint. They wanted this crate. They were making me load it onto the dolly...and that's when you came by."

"None of that's true," Rev said. "Those two were the ones trying to get the crate out of here. The stolen mummy case is in it."

The guard's gaze slowly swept the four of us. "Well," he said at last, "anybody trying to steal anything's for the police to sort out. So I'm just going to buzz the office now, get this called in."

Still holding the two guns, he began moving sideways.

I hadn't noticed earlier, but there was a phone sitting on the end of a workbench.

He put Rev's gun onto the bench and reached for the receiver.

Then, in the blink of an eye, a man stepped from behind a crate and brought something crashing down on the guard's head.

With a grunt, he crumpled to the floor.

The man who'd hit him tossed aside the crowbar he'd wielded, grabbed the gun from the bench, then quickly crouched and took the second one from where the guard had dropped it.

As he stood up again, Rev breathed in sharply, making me look at him.

He was staring at the man in shocked recognition.

I glanced across the room again. The newcomer's eyes were fixed on Rev. His expression also said they knew each other. But I didn't have a clue who he was.

"You should shoot them," Rachel said to him. "Right now."

"Sure," he snapped. "And have the rest of security down here the minute they hear the shots? *I'll* worry about what to do with these two. You go check that the the coast's still clear."

Rachel didn't argue, simply turned and darted out of the room. Whoever this newcomer was, he was obviously in charge.

"You," he said, pointing one of the guns at Rev. "Help Usher get that crate on the dolly. Fast."

"And you," he went on, turning to me when Rev and Scott began wrestling with the crate. "Move. Over there, where I can see you."

I moved, trying to look as frightened and innocent as possible. Frightened was no effort at all. Innocent took more work. I was so aware of my own gun digging into my waist that if this guy was the slightest bit psychic, he'd realize it was hidden there.

"Okay," he muttered when I'd walked about six feet past the others. "There's good. Now stay where you are."

The way my adrenaline was pumping I could barely stand still, but I didn't want to make even the slightest movement. Nothing to draw his attention back to me. I just had to wait for my chance and get my gun out and shoot him . . . if I could actually force myself to.

I'd have to, though. Because I knew that if I didn't, he'd kill Rev and me the minute he wasn't worried about the noise.

He stood watching Rev and Scott ease the crate onto the dolly. I stood watching him, trying to figure out who he could be. He was in his mid-thirties, tall and dark. A really good-looking man if you go for the Sylvester Stallone type.

I was certain I'd never seen him before. But Rev had. There'd been no misreading the initial look that had passed between them.

"That's it," Scott said.

I glanced back at Rev and Scott. They had the crate fully on the dolly.

A second later, Rachel raced back into the room, her face flushed. "The lights are on in receiving and two security guards are looking around there. Someone must have realized we put the alarm system out of commission."

"All right," the man said. "We'll go out that big side exit and bring the wagon around to it. You," he said to me. "You go first." He gestured toward a dark section of the far wall.

For a moment, I couldn't see what he was pointing at. Then I realized there was a second door in the room, almost completely concealed by stacked cartons and a couple of large trunks standing on end.

My heart pounding, I started forward. It was now or never. If they got Rev and me away from the museum we'd be goners.

As I neared the cartons I feigned a stumble and banged into the stack with all my weight.

The boxes toppled like building blocks. I dove for the cover of the trunks. Gunshots began blasting, their echoes thundering around the room.

I dug my gun from under my sweatshirt and reached around the trunks, firing in the man's general direction.

I kept pulling the trigger. I couldn't hit someone I couldn't even see, but the more noise the better. And this noise was deafening. Like being on a firing range without ear-protectors. The air was growing thick with the smell of gunpowder.

Then my gun clicked empty.

The silence had barely registered before more cartons were crashing down to my left. I whirled around. This time the man had knocked them over in his race for the door.

"Cover Scott and Rachel," Rev shouted, running by me in pursuit.

Frantically, I looked around for them. They were huddled together beneath a workbench. I scrambled to my feet and aimed my empty gun at them, saying, "Stay right there. Move and you're dead."

IT COULDN'T HAVE BEEN two minutes before there were half a dozen security guards in the workroom, all with their guns drawn. The shooting had attracted everyone on duty.

The first one to arrive had phoned in the emergency, asking for both the police and an ambulance.

The fellow who'd been bashed with the crowbar looked terrible, his head and face covered in blood. But he'd regained consciousness, which I knew was a good sign.

When the second guard had raced in, I'd grabbed his arm and pointed at Scott and Rachel, saying, "I know he works here, but they're crooks. Don't let them out of this room."

The man had started to ask me something, but I'd waved him off, explaining only that I was out of rounds.

As the room filled, I anxiously watched the doorway that Rev had chased our mystery man through.

Finally, unable to stand the waiting any longer, I picked my way among the scattered cartons and walked out into the hallway beyond. Luckily the guards had met me during the investigation, so they knew I was a "good guy" and let me go.

The darkness gave me serious pause, but if Rev came waltzing back into the workroom unannounced, one of those security guards was liable to get trigger-happy.

Uneasily, I started down the almost-black hall. It seemed to stretch for miles, and when I finally reached an intersecting corridor I stopped and ran my hand along the wall, desperately hoping to find a light switch.

And then I heard the faint sound of squeaky footsteps.

"Rev?" I called, realizing only as I said his name that it might be the other man I'd heard.

"Yeah, it's me," Rev called back.

My momentary panic vanished. I hurried in the direction of his voice, throwing myself into his arms when I reached him.

"You okay?" he whispered, hugging me tightly.

"Fine. You?"

He kissed me. A long, deep kiss that told me just how fine he was.

When he stopped, I drew his lips back to mine once more. We had to do *something* while we were waiting for the police to arrive. And standing in the dark, kissing Revington York, had a lot more to commend it than standing around in a room full of museum security guards.

Finally, I rested my cheek against the warmth of his chest, listening to the solid, reassuring beating of his heart. "Everything's going to be okay now, isn't it," I murmured.

"Isn't it?" I repeated when he didn't reply.

"I don't know, Marina. Things aren't over yet. I lost that guy in the dark and couldn't figure which way the side exit was. He's probably halfway out of the city by now."

"Who was he?"

"No idea."

"But I thought you recognized him. I—" Suddenly, the lights flashed on, both blinding and terrifying.

Rev whirled around, swinging me into the wall and protecting me with his body.

"Hey!" a man called. "Hey, relax. It's me. Frank Barboni."

He strolled toward us, a broad grin on his face.

"What are you doing here?" I asked. "We didn't think you'd be on duty tonight."

"I'm not. But I was in my office, catching up on some paperwork, when the call came in over the radio. So I commandeered a cruiser. But what *I'm* doing here is hardly the question. I should arrest you two. I told you to stay away from this place."

"You meant at night, too?" Rev said. "Hell, we didn't realize that, did we, Marina?"

I simply smiled at him.

"Civilians," Barboni muttered, not quite managing to look angry. "So, what happened here?"

Quickly, we filled him in.

"There was no Magic Wagon out back when we got here," Barboni said once we were done. "Only a car. But we'll put out a bulletin on the wagon. And on the guy, once we know who he is."

We headed back to the workroom. While we'd been gone, it had emptied. Only two uniformed cops were there now, one standing at each door.

Rachel and Scott had been taken to a couple of the museum's offices for interrogation. The injured guard was on his way to hospital.

The wooden crate was still standing on the dolly. I walked over to it and ran my hand along the wood, searching for bullet holes, praying there weren't any. As far as I could tell, it hadn't been hit.

"So the mummy case is in there, huh?" Barboni said.

"I think it *has* to be," Rev said.

"We'd better open the crate. Make sure." Barboni gestured for the two uniformed cops to get started.

They set the crate flat on the floor and grabbed a couple of crowbars. I hovered anxiously, telling them to be careful.

Finally, they got the top pried off. Inside, shipping blankets were wrapped carefully around the contents.

The cops backed off a couple of steps, even though they were obviously curious, and Barboni folded back the quilting, exposing the beauty of the mummy case.

I gazed at it, certain I was looking at the real thing.

"You were right," Rev told me quietly. "She does look like you."

My eyes lingered on Princess Amonit's painted face for another moment. Then my gaze flickered down the entire length of the wooden human shape.

"Lord," one of the cops muttered, "the papers said the thing was priceless, but I didn't expect this. Look at those jewels. And all that gold."

My neck had begun growing strangely warm. I lifted my hair off the back of it, but that didn't help. Then I realized the sensation of heat was coming from the mummy beads, tucked under my sweatshirt.

"We should open the case itself," I said, not even thinking before I spoke. There was no doubt in my mind that was what we had to do.

"We'd better wait for someone from the museum," Barboni said.

"No...no, we've got to do it now." I glanced at Rev, feeling like an idiot, but something was making me insist. Or, rather, *someone* was making me insist.

Rev merely nodded. He understood. "I know how these cases were fastened together," he told Barboni. "We can open it without doing any damage."

"Uh-uh. Not with that ancient mummy inside and all."

"I know what I'm doing," Rev persisted. "Really, I transport art all the time. And my business depends on the pieces never being damaged." He pushed more of the quilting away from the mummy case. "See? All that's holding the top on are these few pins on either side."

He glanced around, then said to one of the cops, "Hand me that, would you? That tool on the workbench?"

It was some sort of artist's chisel, and it helped Rev remove the pins with far less effort than I'd have expected. Or maybe, I thought with a tiny shiver, he was getting help from more than the chisel.

"There," he said, easing the last pin out and putting it carefully down with the others. "Now, if somebody would just take the other end . . . the top alone won't be all that heavy to lift."

Barboni clearly wasn't having any part of the venture, but one of the cops volunteered.

"Okay," Rev said, putting his hands gently on either side of the painted wooden head. "Lift on three. Up and toward the wall. One . . . two . . . three."

They shifted the top off the mummy case.

"Oh, my God," I whispered.

The case was empty. Princess Amonit's mummy wasn't inside.

Chapter Fifteen

It was well past one in the morning before Frank Barboni finished taking statements from me, then Rev. After the two of them were done, Barboni went off to talk to the detectives who'd been questioning Rachel and Scott.

"If you want to wait," he told us before he left, "I'll let you know as much as I can."

Exhausted as we were, we waited in the museum's lounge. There were a million blanks we wanted filled in. Most important, to me at least, was learning what had happened to Princess Amonit's mummy. I wanted to know it was safe and sound. And that it would end up back in the mummy case, where it belonged.

By the time Barboni returned I was half asleep, curled up on a couch with my head in Rev's lap. Sitting up straight was a major effort.

"Well," Barboni said, sinking into a chair, "Rachel isn't being very cooperative, but Scott Usher has been singing like a bird."

"And he knew where the mummy is?" I asked.

"I'm afraid not. Both he and Rachel swear they thought it was still in the case. They figure Joe must have done something with it."

"Joe?" Rev said.

"Joe Callivetti," Barboni told him. "That's who the other guy was tonight. The one who got away."

It took a second for the name to click into place. "The boyfriend," I said when it did. "Janet Koslovsky's boyfriend. A restorer at the museum, right?"

"Right. And the story Scott and Rachel tell has him as both the brains behind the scheme and Janet's murderer."

"What about Ashton Crawly?" Rev asked.

"Apparently, we had him pegged wrong."

I shook my head. "You know, Scott went on to Rev and me about not wanting to repeat gossip. But then he told us everything people were saying about Crawly, anyway. I guess he figured we'd never suspect him if we all were sure Crawly was guilty."

"The only thing he was actually guilty of was having an affair with Janet," Barboni said. "And when Callivetti found out about that, he killed her."

"For cheating on him," I said, my stomach feeling queasy. Even though I'd never met Janet . . .

"He told Scott he killed her in a fit of rage," Barboni said. "But that's not true. Not when he thought to make her phone Crawly first and give him that story about heading off to the Caribbean. Actually, it seems he was more worried she might know something and would start to confide in Crawly. Or maybe she *did* catch on to his scheme and threatened to tell the authorities."

"But why did he mummify her?" Rev asked.

Barboni shrugged. "The guy has a macabre sense of humor. He had to get rid of the body somehow, and he figured that putting a phony mummy in the phony case would be funny."

"Hilarious," I muttered.

"According to Scott, Joe called it *adding authenticity*."

"Joe Callivetti isn't his real name, is it," Rev said.

I glanced at him, recalling the look of recognition I'd seen pass between them.

"Maybe not," Barboni said. "We haven't had time to run a check on his prints yet. But even if Callivetti *is* an alias, he shouldn't be hard to ID. There can't be many guys in the country with the talent to make a reproduction like the one he made."

"So he was the one with the skill," I murmured. "And he came up with the plan, as well."

"Right. He met Scott when he started working at the Donner, and met Rachel through Scott. Then, when he heard that Careful Wheels was going to be transporting the exhibit, he saw a way of making them all rich."

"And Scott and Rachel went right along with him," Rev said. "Hell, I'm sure a terrific judge of character. I thought Scott was a nice guy, and I gave Rachel a job."

"You never know about people," Barboni said. "And you might not have been too far off base about Scott. He seems like a basically nice guy who just got too interested in big bucks. He claims he didn't want any part of the idea at first, but Rachel finally convinced him by... you're going to love this one, Rev. Rachel figured they could get away with it by framing *you*. Make us think you switched the cases while the exhibit was being transported. Scott claims they sent you some beads that would eventually have incriminated you. Beads from the real mummy. You get anything like that?"

My heart racing, I rested my hand on the mummy beads beneath my sweatshirt. I knew I couldn't keep them. Not forever. But somehow I knew I couldn't give them up just yet. I glanced at Rev, sending him a silent message.

"*Some* beads were delivered," he said slowly. "But the note with them said they were reproductions from the museum's gift shop. I gave them to Marina...she even wore them once or twice."

"Probably they really were reproductions," Barboni said. "But Scott says that the top few strips of linen wrapping on the mummy had rotted away. The necklace was exposed, and Rachel decided...well, we'll worry about whether the story's true or not some other time. Anything else that needs filling in?"

"The car bombs?" I said.

"Oh, yeah. Callivetti, whoever he really is, knows explosives. And they got worried that Charlie Obregon was asking so many questions he was bound to come across the answers. And then you, Marina...well, you were causing them all kinds of confusion. First, they didn't know what you'd learned in L.A., so that was when they tried to blow up your car. Then, Rachel saw you wearing the beads that were supposed to have framed Rev..."

Barboni paused and scratched his head. I knew he'd realized there was something he was missing about the beads but hadn't quite figured out what, yet.

"At any rate," he went on, "they realized Rev was working *with* you. So then they decided they'd be wise to bump off both of you. They didn't tell us a whole lot of details about that, but they seemed to have had plots on top of their plots."

"Like the snake," I said. "And the scorpion."

"Yeah, but those were really just weird scare tactics. The canary disappearing, too. Rachel let it out the window."

I nodded, glad to hear she hadn't killed Tweetie. Not that his chances of surviving in the world would be very great, but maybe somebody had realized he was a pet and taken him in.

"If they couldn't manage to kill you, they at least wanted to convince the two of you to back off," Barboni added.

"They almost succeeded," I admitted.

"Well... I guess, unless you've got any more questions, that's it. We'll track Callivetti down. And when we do we'll get the mummy back. It may not be as valuable as the case, but with all those amulets and things in the wrappings it's still worth a small fortune. It'll be stashed someplace safe. At any rate, as far as you two are concerned, the excitement is over."

"Almost," a quiet, silvery voice whispered in my ear. "Almost, but not quite."

AT REV'S SUGGESTION, we went back to my apartment rather than his. I half expected to feel nervous when I opened the door, but I didn't.

It felt good to be home. Even the dark nooks and crannies seemed welcoming. And when Rev wrapped his arms around me and kissed me, everything was perfect.

"Want me to go home?" he murmured at last, his breath warm against my throat.

"What do you think I want?" I teased, smoothing my hands up beneath his sweatshirt.

"Oh... I think maybe you want to sit on the couch for a bit... talk."

Neither the couch nor talk was what I'd had in mind, but I could tell that something was bothering him.

For all that talking had been *his* suggestion, though, once we were snuggled on the couch he didn't say a word.

I didn't press him, simply sat trying to put Princess Amonit's last little message out of my mind. I didn't like the idea of the excitement not being quite over for Rev and me. We'd had enough excitement to last a lifetime.

I wanted the mummy recovered, of course. But it would be, without any more help from Rev and me. The police would find Joe Callivetti, whoever he really was. And when they did, they'd get the mummy back and the princess's spirit would be at rest.

Absently, I put my hand on the mummy beads, recalling the feeling I'd had earlier, when Barboni had asked Rev about them. I should have handed them over, right then and there. Why had it seemed so important that I keep them for just a little longer?

"Do not worry about that," the silvery voice murmured. "They will let you keep the beads forever, Marina. As a reward for finding my mummy case. They will let you keep them because I will tell them they must."

I couldn't help smiling at that. This time, Princess Amonit was wrong. Even *she* couldn't have enough influence to see that beads as valuable as these ones would simply be given away.

"What are you thinking about?" Rev asked.

"Princess Amonit."

He shook his head. "Between those beads, her voice and her *ba,* she gave us a pretty strange time. But if it hadn't been for the mummy case, we'd never have met."

"It was worth the strange time," I murmured, resting my head on his shoulder.

I couldn't conceive of never having met Revington York. No more than I could conceive of ever being without him now that we *had* met. My mother always told me that when I found the right man, I'd know. I was never going to doubt her again.

"So?" I said after a minute. "Do you think Barboni was right? That whoever Joe Callivetti really is, he shouldn't be hard to find?"

"That isn't exactly what Barboni said. He said the guy shouldn't be hard to *ID*. I have a feeling that finding him will be another story."

"Why?"

"I . . . it's just a feeling."

"You don't have a feeling about him bothering us anymore, do you?"

"No. No, he won't bother us, Marina. I wouldn't let him."

"Rev?" I murmured when he didn't go on. "Rev . . . you know who Joe Callivetti really is, don't you? You recognized him."

"No, I didn't."

"But I thought . . . the way the two of you looked at each other . . . I was sure."

"Anyone ever tell you that you have the world's most active imagination?"

"Well, yes, but—"

He cut me off with a kiss that was so passionate I forgot what we'd been talking about.

"Don't you think it's bedtime?" I whispered at last.

"Yes. But there's something I have to tell you first."

"What?"

"Just that . . . I love you, Marina. And I'm never going to stop loving you. Not for as long as I live. I . . . I just
want you to know that."

"I love you too, Rev," I whispered, tracing his lips
with my fingers. "I love you so much it scares me."

"Don't be scared." He wrapped his arms tightly
around me and kissed the top of my head. "I don't want
you ever to be scared again. I'll do anything it takes to
keep you safe."

WHEN I WOKE in the morning, the first thing I thought
about was Rev. He was gone from the bed, but his scent
lingered on my pillow.

The second thing I thought about was that it was
Saturday. We had two whole days to spend alone together.

The apartment was silent, and there was no answer
when I called him, so I put on a robe and wandered out
of the bedroom to find him.

He wasn't there to be found, and his car keys weren't
on the end table where he'd left them last night.

I decided he'd gone out to get things for breakfast.
Given the empty state of my fridge, that had been a
good idea.

When he wasn't back by the time I'd showered and
dressed, I was a little worried. By the time I'd made
enough coffee for both of us and drunk the entire pot
myself, I was a lot worried. If he'd intended to be gone
this long, wouldn't he have left a note?

I called his apartment, got his answering machine and
left a message. Then I tried Careful Wheels and got the
machine there, as well. I didn't get a connection calling
his car phone, so it was probably unplugged.

The more time that passed, the more certain I grew that something awful had happened to him. Finally, I dug the keys to his apartment out of my bag, glad he'd insisted on giving them to me, and headed over to his place.

People always talk about accidents in the home, so I'd check that possibility first. If he wasn't lying dead on his living room floor, I'd start phoning hospitals.

Leaving my car illegally parked in front of his building, the way Rev, himself, would have done, I hurried upstairs. I was so anxious I had trouble getting the key into the lock. When I finally opened the door, there was no dead body in sight.

Nervously, I looked through the entire apartment. There was no dead body anywhere. No live one, either. I checked his machine, but the only message on it was mine. It was time to start calling hospitals.

I pulled out the desk drawer, looking for a phone book, but there wasn't one. There was another phone beside his bed, so I went into the bedroom and checked the drawer of the bedside table. Again, I came up empty.

Thinking there might be shelves in the closet, I slid open the door... and stood staring at space.

Aside from a robe that had seen better days, a few lonely shirts and a pair of sneakers so worn the toes were half-gone, the closet was empty.

Not quite able to believe my eyes, I opened a dresser drawer. Almost empty. As was the next one. And the bottom one.

I sank onto the bed, my mind reeling. Revington York had gone somewhere. Without a word about it to me.

I SPENT THE ENTIRE DAY in a state of shock and anxiety, waiting to hear from Rev. This man I'd fallen desperately in love with, who'd said he loved me, too—who'd said he'd never stop loving me as long as he lived—had disappeared.

There had to be an explanation. Something urgent had come up. But what could be so urgent that he hadn't taken time to call me? Especially when he'd taken time to pack?

By four o'clock I was frantic. Then someone buzzed my apartment.

I raced across the living room, so certain it was Rev downstairs that I didn't take time to ask, simply buzzed him in, then opened my apartment door and headed to the stairs to meet him.

The man coming up the staircase wasn't Rev, though. It was Frank Barboni.

I tried to hide my disappointment and smile a greeting, but it didn't feel like much of a smile. It couldn't have looked like much of one, either, because he didn't smile back, just asked if he could come in for a minute.

"Marina," he said soberly, once we were sitting in the living room, "they asked me to come by personally and tell you something."

Impatiently, I nodded. Under different circumstances, I'd be interested in hearing whatever he'd come to tell me about his investigation, but at the moment all I was interested in was hearing from Rev.

"There's been a plane crash, Marina. A small private plane. It went down in the Sierra Nevadas."

I eyed him uncertainly.

"Ahh...we don't have any details," he went on, running his fingers through his hair. "But the pilot and passenger were both killed. Marina... Rev was the passenger on that plane. I'm sorry."

The words didn't sink in at first. I simply sat staring blankly at Frank Barboni, not understanding.

"I'm sorry," he said again. "If there's anything the department can do..."

"There's been a mistake," I said, a rush of relief sweeping me as I realized that's what had happened. "There's been a mistake."

"No...no mistake. I wish that was it. But Rev's Porsche was left at the airstrip. A mechanic talked to him about its engine...walked him to the plane. They showed the guy a picture of Rev...he was definitely the passenger."

Slowly, a shroud of unspeakable anguish wrapped itself around me. My body began to shake with silent sobs.

Revington York was the man I loved. If he was dead, I didn't want to live.

VOICE
OF THE
NILE

continues in February with...

THE
MUMMY
BEADS

The mysterious silvery voice speaks again, so turn this page and listen, because Princess Amonit has startling news for Marina... the man she loves is out there somewhere—alive!

Prologue

The man she adored was kissing her. A deep, lingering kiss that made her happier than she'd ever imagined possible.

"I'll never stop loving you," he murmured, his breath caressing her lips.

Marina reached to trace the line of his jaw with her fingertips. But instead of his warm skin, all she felt was a cool cotton pillowcase.

Instantly, the fullness of love became the emptiness of reality. She was alone in bed. Alone, cold, and wide awake in the darkness.

She switched on the bedside lamp and gazed at Rev's photograph, wishing it could speak. If it could only tell her the truth about what had happened...but his death, like his life, had been surrounded in mystery.

When she'd tried to learn the details, it had seemed as if a stone wall of secrecy had been thrown up.

Even the news coverage had been minimal, adding nothing to what Detective Barboni had told her. A small private plane had crashed somewhere in the Sierra Nevadas. Only the pilot and Revington York were aboard. Both were killed.

He'd left her bed while she was sound asleep, then boarded the plane. Without a word about what he was doing or where he was going.

She knew he'd have called to explain. He'd loved her too much to have left her worrying for long. If only he'd reached his destination, he would have called.

But the way things had turned out, she'd never know where he was going or why he'd left so suddenly...what it was that had led him to his death.

Wiping away a few stray tears, she got out of bed and put on her robe. Trying to go back to sleep would be pointless. She had a year's experience to tell her that. And her reflection, in the dresser mirror, showed the effect of all those months of sleepless nights.

She looked even worse than her passport photo. It was obvious why her parents were worried about her. Why they'd begun gently prodding her to start getting on with her life.

Deep down, she knew that sooner or later she'd have to. She was only twenty-nine. She could hardly go on this way for another fifty or sixty years.

Slowly, she pulled open the top dresser drawer, then dug under her lingerie for the black velvet box that held the beads from Princess Amonit's mummy.

The day Rev had been killed, she'd taken them off and put them away. They'd been too painful to even look at, because they were so much a part of the incredible adventure that she'd shared with him.

She opened the box and gazed at them, still not quite able to believe the priceless necklace now belonged to her.

Closing her eyes, she could recall Princess Amonit's voice saying, "They will let you keep the beads forever, Marina. As a reward for finding my mummy case. They will let you keep them because I will tell them they must.''

At the time, she hadn't believed the princess. She had been certain the beads were far too valuable for someone to part with. But she should have known better than to doubt anything a three-thousand-year-old spirit said.

The man who owned the mummy case, who'd lent it to the museum, *had* insisted Marina keep the ancient beads as a reward.

Lightly, she ran her fingers along them. Six strands, each strung in the same pattern of navy, red and turquoise colored beads. With three little gold charms hanging from the bottom strand. The fish amulet, to prevent drowning. The cowrie shell, representing the wish to have children. And the little figure of Heh, the god who symbolized long life.

She remembered the first time she'd seen the beads. Remembered Rev saying, "Try them on...they look great on you.''

Hesitantly, she took them from the velvet box. Maybe it was time to put her demons to rest.

She fastened the necklace in place and stood gazing into the mirror.

Then, for the first time in over a year, she heard Princess Amonit's silvery voice.

"I have been waiting for you, Marina," it murmured. "Waiting for you to be ready. Because the man you love is not dead at all. And he still loves you as much as ever. I will help you find him if you wish.''

Her entire body began to tremble. It was all she could do to whisper, "Yes. Oh, yes, I *do* wish.''

"Good. And when that is done, the two of you will help find my soul's resting place...my mummy. I must have both of you to assist me. And you will make this covenant with me, Marina? This bargain?''

"Of course," she whispered, still shaking. She'd make *any* bargain to find Rev.

"Good," the princess said again. "Because only when there is a place for my spirit to dwell will it have eternal peace."

Marina sank onto the bed. The man she loved wasn't dead. And he still loved her. She knew she could believe Princess Amonit.

But if what the princess said was true, why hadn't Rev been in contact with her?

Because someone had prevented it? Because he'd been injured, or was in terrible trouble?

Whatever the answer, Marina had to find him. And to do that, she'd go wherever Princess Amonit led.

To find Revington York, she'd go to the ends of the earth.

* * * * *

Don't miss this next tale of romance and suspense . . .
THE MUMMY BEADS
February Intrigue #261
Revington York loved Marina . . . but why did he leave, and can Marina ever forgive?

OFFICIAL RULES • MILLION DOLLAR SWEEPSTAKES
NO PURCHASE OR OBLIGATION NECESSARY TO ENTER

To enter, follow the directions published. **ALTERNATE MEANS OF ENTRY:** Hand print your name and address on a 3"x5" card and mail to either: Harlequin "Match 3," 3010 Walden Ave., P.O. Box 1867, Buffalo, NY 14269-1867, or Harlequin "Match 3," P.O. Box 609, Fort Erie, Ontario L2A 5X3, and we will assign your Sweepstakes numbers. (Limit: one entry per envelope.) For eligibility, entries must be received no later than March 31, 1994. No responsibility is assumed for lost, late or misdirected entries.

Upon receipt of entry, Sweepstakes numbers will be assigned. To determine winners, Sweepstakes numbers will be compared against a list of randomly preselected prizewinning numbers. In the event all prizes are not claimed via the return of prizewinning numbers, random drawings will be held from among all other entries received to award unclaimed prizes.

Prizewinners will be determined no later than May 30, 1994. Selection of winning numbers and random drawings are under the supervision of D.L. Blair, Inc., an independent judging organization, whose decisions are final. One prize to a family or organization. No substitution will be made for any prize, except as offered. Taxes and duties on all prizes are the sole responsibility of winners. Winners will be notified by mail. Chances of winning are determined by the number of entries distributed and received.

Sweepstakes open to persons 18 years of age or older, except employees and immediate family members of Torstar Corporation, D.L. Blair, Inc., their affiliates, subsidiaries and all other agencies, entities and persons connected with the use, marketing or conduct of this Sweepstakes. All applicable laws and regulations apply. Sweepstakes offer void wherever prohibited by law. Any litigation within the province of Quebec respecting the conduct and awarding of a prize in this Sweepstakes must be submitted to the Régies des Loteries et Courses du Quebec. In order to win a prize, residents of Canada will be required to correctly answer a time-limited arithmetical skill-testing question. Values of all prizes are in U.S. currency.

Winners of major prizes will be obligated to sign and return an affidavit of eligibility and release of liability within 30 days of notification. In the event of non-compliance within this time period, prize may be awarded to an alternate winner. Any prize or prize notification returned as undeliverable will result in the awarding of that prize to an alternate winner. By acceptance of their prize, winners consent to use of their names, photographs or other likenesses for purposes of advertising, trade and promotion on behalf of Torstar Corporation without further compensation, unless prohibited by law.

This Sweepstakes is presented by Torstar Corporation, its subsidiaries and affiliates in conjunction with book, merchandise and/or product offerings. Prizes are as follows: Grand Prize–$1,000,000 (payable at $33,333.33 a year for 30 years). First through Sixth Prizes may be presented in different creative executions, each with the following approximate values: First Prize–$35,000; Second Prize–$10,000; 2 Third Prizes–$5,000 each; 5 Fourth Prizes–$1,000 each; 10 Fifth Prizes–$250 each; 1,000 Sixth Prizes–$100 each. Prizewinners will have the opportunity of selecting any prize offered for that level. A travel-prize option, if offered and selected by winner, must be completed within 12 months of selection and is subject to hotel and flight accommodations availability. Torstar Corporation may present this Sweepstakes utilizing names other than Million Dollar Sweepstakes. For a current list of all prize options offered within prize levels and all names the Sweepstakes may utilize, send a self-addressed, stamped envelope (WA residents need not affix return postage) to: Million Dollar Sweepstakes Prize Options/Names, P.O. Box 4710, Blair, NE 68009.

The Extra Bonus Prize will be awarded in a random drawing to be conducted no later than May 30, 1994 from among all entries received. To qualify, entries must be received by March 31, 1994 and comply with published directions. No purchase necessary. For complete rules, send a self-addressed, stamped envelope (WA residents need not affix return postage) to: Extra Bonus Prize Rules, P.O. Box 4600, Blair, NE 68009.

For a list of prizewinners (available after July 31, 1994) send a separate, stamped, self-addressed envelope to: Million Dollar Sweepstakes Winners, P.O. Box 4728, Blair, NE 68009.   SWP-H12/93

Valentine's Day was the best day of the year for
Dee's Candy and Gift Shop. Yet as the day drew closer,
Deanna Donovan became the target of
malicious, anonymous pranks.

A red heart was pinned to her front door with a dagger.

Dead roses adorned her car.

Soon, she was being stalked by her unseen admirer.

Suspicious of everyone, Deanna has nowhere to turn—and no
way to escape when she is kidnapped and held captive by her
Valentine lover....

#262

Cupid's Dagger
by *Leona Karr*
February 1994

You'll never again think of Valentine's Day without feeling a
thrill of delight...and a chill of dread!   CUPID

My Valentine
1994

Celebrate the most romantic day of the year with
MY VALENTINE 1994
a collection *of original stories, written by*
four of Harlequin's most popular authors...

MARGOT DALTON
MURIEL JENSEN
MARISA CARROLL
KAREN YOUNG

Available in February, wherever
Harlequin Books are sold.

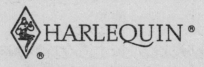

HARLEQUIN ®

VAL94

NEW YORK TIMES Bestselling Author

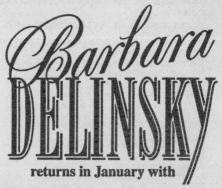

Barbara DELINSKY

returns in January with

THE REAL THING

Stranded on an island off the coast of Maine,
Deirdre Joyce and Neil Hersey got the
solitude they so desperately craved—
but they also got each other, something they
hadn't expected. Nor had they expected
to be consumed by a desire so powerful
that the idea of living alone again was
unimaginable. A marrige of "convenience"
made sense—or did it?   BOB7

HARLEQUIN®

HARLEQUIN®

Don't miss these Harlequin favorites by some of our most distinguished authors!
And now, you can receive a discount by ordering two or more titles!

Harlequin Promotional Titles

(short-story collection featuring Anne Stuart, Judith Arnold,
Anne McAllister, Linda Randall Wisdom)
(limited quantities available on certain titles)

	AMOUNT	$
DEDUCT:	**10% DISCOUNT FOR 2+ BOOKS**	$
ADD:	**POSTAGE & HANDLING**	$
	($1.00 for one book, 50¢ for each additional)	
	APPLICABLE TAXES*	$ _____
	TOTAL PAYABLE	$ _____
	(check or money order—please do not send cash)	

To order, complete this form and send it, along with a check or money order for the total above, payable to Harlequin Books, to: **In the U.S.:** 3010 Walden Avenue, P.O. Box 9047, Buffalo, NY 14269-9047; **In Canada:** P.O. Box 613, Fort Erie, Ontario, L2A 5X3.

Name: _____

Address: _____ City: _____

State/Prov.: _____ Zip/Postal Code: _____

*New York residents remit applicable sales taxes.
 Canadian residents remit applicable GST and provincial taxes.

HBACK-JM